World Elite DANCE ACADEMY

BILLIE'S BIG AUDITION

Kimberly Wyatt

EGMONT

EGMONT

We bring stories to life

First published in Great Britain 2017
by Egmont UK Limited
The Yellow Building, 1 Nicholas Road, London W11 4AN

Text copyright © 2017 Beautiful Movements Ltd
Cover illustration copyright © 2017 Beautiful Movements Ltd
Written in collaboration with Siobhan Curham

The moral rights of the author and illustrator have been asserted

ISBN 978 1 4052 8717 3

67251/3

A CIP catalogue record for this title is available
from the British Library

Typeset by Avon DataSet Ltd, Bidford on Avon, Warwickshire

Printed and bound in Great Britain by the CPI Group

Stay safe online. Any website addresses listed in this book are correct at the time
of going to print. However, Egmont is not responsible for content hosted by third
parties. Please be aware that online content can be subject to change and websites
can contain content that is unsuitable for children. We advise that all children
are supervised when using the internet.

MIX
Paper
FSC FSC® C018306

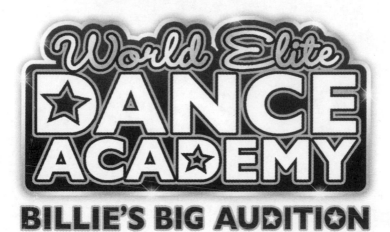

BILLIE'S BIG AUDITION

To Ms Jo, Ms Stephanie, Ms Bonnie,
Ms Heidi, Ms Kathy and the WODA family

CHAPTER ONE

'*Five, six, seven, eight . . .*' Billie held her partner tightly as she leaned into an arabesque. In her mind she was beneath a golden spotlight at the Royal Opera House with the famous ballet dancer, Rudolph Nureyev. In reality she was dancing beneath a flickering strip light in an office building . . . with a bin. '*Drop, six, seven, eight.*' She lowered the wastepaper basket and tipped its contents into the huge bin bag at her feet. Dancing around was the only thing that made helping out at her mum's cleaning job bearable. At the other end of the office, Billie's mum, her golden hair tied back in a red bandana, was humming her favourite Jill Scott song, 'A Long Walk'. The regulars in the cafe where Billie's mum worked called her 'the songbird'. Her mum loved singing as much as Billie loved dancing, and it helped her in the same way, too.

Billie squirted some polish on the desk in front of her. She wondered if the people who worked in this office ever thought about who cleaned up after them every night. She doubted it. She rubbed the polish into the desk until all the rings from the coffee cups had disappeared and the wood began to shine. As she polished, her mind returned to her feet and she ran through a sequence of steps in time to the song her mum was singing. This was how it always was – her mind constantly being pulled back to dance. As she pushed a wheeled chair back into place, she pretended it was Nureyev, holding her tight, about to raise her into the most beautiful lift the ballet world had ever seen. Higher and higher and . . . *CRASH*. The wheels on Chair-Nureyev buckled and it collided with the desk.

'Careful!' her mum called. 'You don't want to injure yourself the night before your big audition.'

Billie gulped. For a brief moment she'd managed to forget about the audition. *What if she messed up? What if she didn't make it? What if her dream came to nothing?*

'Uh-oh.' Kate came down the office dragging a vacuum cleaner behind her. 'Looks like someone's having an attack of the *what-ifs*.'

Billie couldn't help laughing. Her mum could read her like a book – even from the other end of an office. And it worked both ways. It had been just the two of them for so long that they knew each other inside out. Like right now, Billie could tell her mum was more tired than usual because the shadows under her eyes were a few shades darker.

She took a deep breath. She couldn't let her mum see her fear, not when she was under so much pressure herself. Billie needed to stay strong. She needed to change the *what-ifs* in her mind to *I-cans. I can pass the audition. I can dance well enough. I can do it.*

'You're going to be amazing, sweetheart,' Kate

said, putting her arm round Billie's shoulders.

Billie leaned into her. 'I can't believe it's tomorrow. For ages it felt like it was never going to happen and now . . .'

'I know. All of a sudden it's here.'

Billie had applied to audition for WEDA – the World Elite Dance Academy – back in January. Her audition letter had arrived in February and had been pinned to the board in their kitchen ever since. It was now the middle of May.

'Come on,' her mum said. 'Let's get this floor hoovered and get out of here. We have a surprise guest coming for dinner.'

'Who?' Billie stared at her. 'Not Uncle Charlie?'

Kate nodded and grinned.

'But I thought he wasn't back from Vietnam till next month!'

'He wasn't supposed to be. But he decided to come home early so he could wish his favourite niece good luck.'

'That's amazing!' Aside from her mum, her

Uncle Charlie was Billie's favourite human being in the entire world. It was impossible to feel anything other than happy when he was around. Billie did a pirouette in celebration.

When they were back home Billie did some stretches at the kitchen table while her mum stirred pasta sauce at the stove. The air filled with the delicious smell of tomatoes and oregano. As Billie stretched up she looked at the dream-board on the wall. This was where she and her mum stuck pictures of their hopes and dreams, for inspiration. Billie's pictures were all dance-related – a black and white print of a pair of ballet shoes, a photo of an airy, sunlit dance studio and, of course, a picture of WEDA that she'd cut from the brochure. Billie looked at the imposing red brick building, with its huge windows like sets of eyes gazing out over the rolling grounds. It reminded her a bit of Hogwarts, but the bit she loved best was the glass-panelled walkway that jutted from the side of the building, leading to the ultra-modern Murphy Wing.

The Murphy Wing was named after Miss Murphy – former world-famous ballerina, now Head of Dance and Wellness at WEDA and Billie's dance hero. Like she'd done a thousand times before, Billie stared at the glass walkway and pictured herself walking along it on the way to a class. Then she glanced at her mum's side of the dream-board and her eyes came to rest on the picture of a quaint little cottage surrounded by wild flowers. It was her mum's biggest dream to own a home of her own. She'd worked so hard to keep a roof over their heads since Billie's dad had died – working two jobs to cover the rent on their council flat and pay for Billie's dance lessons. Billie felt a flicker of determination deep inside of her. If she got into WEDA and made it as a professional ballerina, she'd one day be able to buy her mum her dream home and take care of her, the way she'd taken care of Billie. She looked at the picture next to the cottage – an old photo of her dad holding two-year-old Billie tightly. His mop of curly hair and his thick-rimmed glasses gave him the look of an earnest college professor. He was staring off to the side of the shot, like he'd just seen something worrying. This photo summed her dad up. He'd devoted his life to finding causes and people to worry about.

The sound of a motorbike growling to a standstill outside snapped Billie from her thoughts. 'Uncle Charlie!'

Billie flung the door open just as Charlie was pulling his helmet from his head.

'Billerina!' he cried, scooping her up into his strong arms. 'How've you been?'

'Great!' Billie replied, breathing in the familiar smell of leather from his jacket. 'It's so good to see you! How was Vietnam?'

'So cool.' Charlie let go of Billie and grinned at her. He looked tanned and healthy – the way he always did when he just got back from travelling. 'The people are so friendly. You'd have loved it. Ah, something smells good.' Charlie followed Billie up the narrow hallway and into the kitchen. 'Hello, Sis. Did you miss me?'

'Charlie!' Billie's mum put down her spoon and grabbed him in a hug.

'I can't believe you're back already,' Billie said, sitting down at the table.

'Yeah well, a little bird told me it was your big day tomorrow, so I had to be here to wish you luck.' Charlie sat down opposite Billie. 'How are you feeling? How are the nerves holding up?'

'OK, I guess.'

'Yeah?' Charlie looked at Billie.

Billie nodded. 'It's just that I've wanted to get into WEDA so badly for so long. I don't know what I'll do if it all goes wrong . . .'

'I get it, but you know what, it can't go wrong, not really, not if you give it your best shot.' Charlie took off his jacket. He had leather bands and colourful, woven friendship bracelets all the way up both of his wrists. Every time he went away he got more.

'But what if –'

'At least you'll have tried,' Charlie interrupted. 'There are two types of people in this world, Bill, the

dreamers and the doers. Us three – and your dad,'
Charlie glanced at the photo on the board, 'we're
doers, right? When we have a dream, we go after it.'

Billie nodded.

'So that's something to be proud of – whatever
the outcome. Anyway, I've got you something.'
Charlie reached inside his jacket pocket.

'From Vietnam?'

'Kind of. I wrote it to you when I was in Vietnam.'
He pulled out a crumpled envelope and handed
it to her. 'Don't open it now. Open it later, when
you're on your own. When you get another attack
of the *what-ifs*.'

Billie tucked the envelope into her hoodie pocket.

'Thank you, Uncle Charlie.'

'No problem, Billerina. Now come on, Sis,
where's our dinner?'

Later that night, when Billie was getting ready for
bed, she took her jewellery box from her dressing
table and opened the lid. She turned the gold key

9

on the back of the box and the little ballerina inside began slowly pirouetting. Billie's dancing dream had begun with this box. It had originally belonged to her mum, who'd had it since she was a child. But when she was little, Billie had become so obsessed with it that her mum let her have it. And when Billie's dad died when she was six, her mum had enrolled Billie in a local dance class, hoping it might help her cope. 'You can be just like the ballerina in the box!' she'd told Billie. And it had worked. In those first years after her dad's death, dancing was the only place where Billie didn't feel as if she was drowning in sadness. In her ballet class there was no time for tears, as she focused on the steps and poses and lost herself in the routines. And, over the seven years since, dancing had gone from being an escape to being a passion.

Billie heard the low murmur of Uncle Charlie's voice from the living room and the light tinkle of her mum's laugh. It was so good hearing her talking to someone, let alone laughing. Her mum spent so many nights alone, worn out from work, slumped in front of her laptop watching Netflix. Billie wished she would meet someone, but her heart still belonged to Billie's dad.

Billie opened the little drawer inside the jewellery box and pulled out a string of wooden beads with a B-shaped pendant. Her dad had given it to her on her sixth birthday, just a few months before he'd died. He'd got it from Africa, where he'd been working in a refugee camp. Billie sighed. He'd been ill when he'd given it to her but no one had known. He'd been so devoted to his work that he didn't bother going to the doctor when he started getting pains in his stomach. He hadn't wanted to let anyone down – and he'd ended up dying. Billie tucked the beads back into the box. She couldn't afford to feel sad tonight – she needed to feel positive for her audition.

She took out a folded magazine cutting. It was about her hero, Miss Murphy. The article charted her incredible rise, from poverty in New York to becoming a scholarship student at WEDA and then one of the most famous and successful dancers in the world. Billie had read the article so many times she practically knew it by heart. As she skim-read it again, her heart began to pound. What if Miss Murphy was at the auditions tomorrow? What if Billie had to dance in front of her? What if she *messed up* in front of her? Her mouth went dry. Then she remembered the envelope Uncle Charlie had given her and fumbled in her pocket for it. She snuggled closer to her bedside lamp and started to read.

If you could take an hour and put it in a glass,
To wait and use it later, when all other time has passed,
If you could take that precious hour and use it for right now,
What would you use it on, knowing time never lasts?
If you could fill that hour with sixty minutes of hope,
If you could know that hour could really come to pass.
Then now is the time to take that hour,
Now is the time to break that glass.

Billie tucked the poem under her pillow, switched off her lamp and closed her eyes. *Now is the time to break that glass*, she repeated over and over in her head until finally she fell asleep.

CHAPTER TWO

Billie got off the train and checked the time on her phone. She went up the station stairs and checked the time on her phone. She emerged blinking into the bright sunlight and checked the time on her phone. But it was no good – she was still crazy early. She'd wanted to give herself time to prepare before everyone else got there, but hadn't meant to be this early. She'd been so worried about something going wrong – the bus not coming, the train being delayed – that she'd set out two hours before she needed to. Of course, for once, everything had been on time.

She started walking along the tree-lined road. WEDA was in a leafy suburb just outside of London, and it was nice being out of the hustle and bustle of the city – the green fields and chirping birds helped soothe Billie's nerves. Following the map on her phone, she turned into the narrow lane that led to the academy. 'I'm a doer, not just a dreamer,' she whispered, reminding herself of Uncle Charlie's pep talk. She had his poem tucked in her pocket for luck too. 'I'm a doer, not just a dreamer.'

The wrought iron gates of the academy loomed into view, and Billie's heart began to pound. *You've got this*, she told herself. *You're going to be great. You're going to dance like a . . . like a fearless tornado!* She grinned. Sometimes her inner motivator said the weirdest things. She slipped through the gate and up the drive, her feet crunching on the gravel. WEDA looked beautiful. The early morning sunlight glowed gold on the glass walls of the Murphy Wing. *This is it*, Billie thought to herself. All the years of practising and training and exams had been leading right up to this moment. She followed the signs to the reception and looked up at the huge wooden doors. What if they were locked?

What if she was so early not even the staff had arrived? But when she gave one of the doors a push it slowly creaked open. Billie stepped into a large reception area. It was cool and dark compared to the bright sunshine outside and smelled of polish.

'Well, someone's ready to slay,' a voice echoed, and she jumped.

Billie turned to see a boy at the other end of the foyer. His dark hair was shaven at the sides and longer and spiky on top. He had latte-coloured skin and was wearing bright orange tracksuit bottoms and a silky black bomber jacket. He was also holding a mop. Billie sighed. Even the cleaners at WEDA had swagger. She suddenly became all too aware of her supermarket trainers and hoodie.

'I take it you're here for the auditions,' the boy said, mopping his way towards her. As he got closer she took in his high cheek bones, full lips, perfectly plucked eyebrows and a smile that lit up the whole room. He was really good-looking – and from the confident way he was leaning on the mop, his other hand on his hip, it looked like he knew it.

'Yes. Sorry I'm so early,' Billie replied. 'I was worried the train was going to be late.'

'And was it?'

'Nope.'

'Ha! Typical.' The boy pursed his lips. 'Why is it that whenever you're early the train's never late? It's like one of those laws of physics – like gravity or something. Go ahead. Make yourself at home.' He gestured to a plush leather sofa on one side of the foyer. 'The receptionist should be here soon. Once it's, you know, not night time any more.' He looked at Billie and burst out laughing. 'Joking. My name's Andre, by the way.'

Billie grinned. 'I'm Billie.' She perched on the edge of the sofa and took a deep breath. WEDA was no longer just a picture on her dream-board. It was real and she was sitting right inside it! She watched Andre as he swished the mop around the floor in large circles. Part of her wished she was back helping her mum in her invisible role as a cleaner. Not that there was anything invisible about Andre; he stood out like a beacon.

Billie was about to take Uncle Charlie's poem from her pocket for a final read when the door crashed open and a girl marched in, followed closely by a woman who Billie guessed must be her mum, judging by their matching manes of dark hair and haughty expressions.

'It's OK, Mum, you can go now,' the girl snapped as she marched straight across Andre's freshly mopped floor.

'Should I not wait until the teachers arrive?' the girl's mum said in a thick Eastern European accent.

'No! I'm fine.'

'No need to shout, Cassandra. Do you have your headshot?'

'Yes.'

'And your CV?'

'Yes!'

'OK, I'll go. But remember everything I told you.'

Cassandra gave a theatrical sigh. 'Yes, Mum.'

As Cassandra's mum turned and swept back out, Andre raised one groomed eyebrow at Billie, who stifled a grin. Cassandra plonked herself down on the sofa, bringing with her a waft of exotic perfume. She smelled as expensive as she looked. Again, Billie looked down at her own clothes and felt a stab of embarrassment. When she'd checked in the mirror before leaving this morning she'd felt fine but now, next to Cassandra with her glossy hair and designer tracksuit, she felt so dull – like an Instagram photo pre-filter.

'Excuse me, cleaner,' Cassandra called to Andre.

Billie watched as Andre's back stiffened and he slowly turned back to face them.

'You talking to me?' he asked.

'Of course. I don't see any other cleaners around here, do you? Unless . . .' She turned to Billie and looked her up and down. 'Are you a cleaner too?'

Billie's heart sank. 'No, I'm here for the audition.'

'Really?' Cassandra sounded so surprised Billie felt even more riddled with self-doubt. 'Well, do either of you know where the toilets are?'

'Third door on the left,' Andre said, pointing his mop in the direction of the corridor. 'Careful you don't get that big head of yours stuck in the door,' he muttered as Cassandra disappeared into the bathroom. Before Billie could respond the door opened and another couple of dancers entered. This was really happening!

Within half an hour the reception area was buzzing with nervous chatter as more and more potential students arrived.

'OK, everyone,' one of the WEDA secretaries called out above the noise. 'Please can you hand in your headshots and CVs at the reception desk then make your way to Studio One in the Murphy Wing. The choreographer will be with you shortly.'

Billie felt a buzz of excitement. They were going to be auditioning in the Murphy Wing! As she made her way along the glass-panelled walkway that linked the two buildings, she felt as if she'd stepped right into her dream-board. In front of her, two girls with perfectly pinned hair and flawless skin chatted to each other excitedly. Billie looked around, hoping to catch a glimpse of Andre cleaning, but he was nowhere to be seen. She sighed. She'd give anything to see a friendly face right now. The other dancers all looked so super-confident. *But they can't be*, she told herself. *WEDA is one of the best dance academies in the world. They must want this as much as you do. They must be just as nervous as you.* Billie followed the others into a huge airy studio and made her way to a space at the front. She still wasn't the fastest at picking up choreography, so it would help to have a good view.

'Got any gum?'

Billie turned and saw a girl behind her. Her eyes were emerald green and her bright magenta hair, in shocking contrast to her snow-white skin, was cut into a sharp bob. She looked kind of fierce. 'What, chewing gum?'

'What other kind of gum is there?'

Billie's face flushed.

'I like to chew before an audition,' the girl explained. 'It helps me release tension.'

'Oh. No, sorry, I don't.'

'I'm Tilly.' She took off her black, boat-necked sweater to reveal a beautiful backless leotard in electric-blue leopard print. Billie looked down at her own faded black leotard. It looked so drab in comparison.

'I'm Billie.'

'Seriously?' Tilly stared at her. 'Billie and Tilly. Jeez, we sound like a comedy duo.'

Tilly began some warm-up stretches. Billie fumbled in her bag for her ballet shoes. They looked so dull and worn under the gleam of the studio lights. Behind her, Tilly started doing the splits. She didn't seem nervous at all. Billie was about to put her shoes on when a boy walked into the studio and headed towards them. There was a noticeable lull in the chatter as all of the girls, and most of the boys, turned to look at him. Billie felt a weird fluttering in the pit of her stomach as the boy came and sat down on the floor next to her. He had olive skin, a mess of curly black hair and dark brown eyes. He was wearing a pale grey vest top and black sweatpants, and had a black beaded necklace with a tiger's eye gemstone around his neck. Rather than warming up like the others, he sat cross-legged and closed his eyes. There was something familiar about him, but Billie didn't know what. She was certain she'd never met him before.

'Wow, check out Buddha here,' Tilly said, a little too loudly, nodding in the boy's direction.

Billie pulled on her ballet shoes and to her horror, her big toe burst through a hole in the tip! Panic churned inside of her. What should she do? She didn't have any other shoes. But how could she dance with one of her toes hanging out? It looked terrible. Billie felt like crying. She was about to audition at WEDA – one of the top dance academies in the world – and there was a massive hole in her shoe!

CHAPTER
THREE

'If I were you, I'd go barefoot,' Tilly said, shuffling closer. 'You won't be able to dance properly like that. You'll be way better barefoot. Take it from someone who knows.'

How did Tilly know? Had she had this happen to her too? But before Billie could say anything, the door opened and a tall, athletic-looking man with cocoa-coloured skin came striding in. Billie took off her shoes and stuffed them in her bag.

'Good morning, everyone,' the man called as he made his way to the front of the studio. He was wearing sweats and a scarf and his feet were encased in socks, legwarmers and sandals, making them look more like a pair of moose's hooves. 'My name's Mr Marlo and I'm going to be your audition choreographer. First of all, can I ask you to place all of your belongings over in the corner behind the piano, then take your positions ready to dance.'

Billie placed her bag in the corner then, as she made her way to the front, Cassandra shoved past her.

'Hey, I was there –' Billie gasped.

'Welcome to WEDA,' Cassandra said with a sneer, before looking down at Billie's bare feet. 'You need to make way for the serious dancers.'

Burning with anger, Billie moved back to the centre of the studio.

'Welcome to the World Elite Dance Academy,' Mr Marlo said, looking around the studio at them all. 'Here at the academy we're looking for dancers willing to work hard, try harder, and aim to be the best in the world. Today's audition will be all about finding those dancers – finding those who have what it takes. This is your chance to shine. To prove yourself. So stay focused and on your game.'

Mr Marlo nodded to an assistant, who tapped on her laptop, filling the studio with classical music. 'Let's start with ballet, beginning with an adage,' Mr Marlo said. 'I'll show you the sequence first, then I want you to join in.'

The next hour passed by in a blur. At first, still shaken from her encounter with Cassandra, Billie felt a little stiff and unsure. But pretty soon she started to relax. Even at WEDA, with so much at stake, she was still able to lose herself in the dance.

'OK, guys, good work,' Mr Marlo said, walking around the studio. When he got to Billie he stopped. 'Where are your shoes?' he asked her quietly.

'One of them broke as I was putting it on. I thought it would be better to dance barefoot,' Billie said, her face flushing.

'I see. Well, good job,' Mr Marlo said, his brown eyes twinkling. 'Your technique could use a little fine-tuning but your determination and attack is impressive. Try to let go of the nerves and surrender to the music even more. I can tell there's a lot of potential in there. Keep up the good work.'

Billie flushed with happiness. A teacher at WEDA had praised her dancing! She looked up and saw Cassandra scowling at her.

Mr Marlo took off his scarf and leaned back against the barre. 'Next, I'm going to call each of you to the front of the studio and I want you to say your name, what you love about dance and three adjectives that best describe you as a person.' He picked up a clipboard. 'OK, first up, let's have Cassandra Ivanov.'

Billie sighed. Typical that Cassandra would get to go first. She watched as Cassandra strode to the front of the studio.

'My name is Cassandra Ivanov and I love to dance because I was born to dance – *obviously*, with my family background.' She looked at Mr Marlo knowingly.

Mr Marlo looked back at her blankly.

'My grandmother danced at the Kirov in Russia. So you could say I'm ballet royalty.'

'Yeah, or you could say you're a stuck-up snob,' Tilly muttered.

Billie bit down on her lip to stop herself laughing. But then her heart sank. What hope did she have competing against someone like Cassandra?

'And could we have three adjectives that best describe you?' Mr Marlo said.

Arrogant, rude, smug? Billie thought.

'Driven, determined, talented,' Cassandra rattled off immediately, like she said it every night in the mirror before she went to sleep.

'OK, now show me what we are working with. I want to see your posture in fifth position. Take four pivots, then go sit over there,' Mr Marlo said, gesturing to the side of the studio. It was slightly reassuring to see that he didn't seem overly impressed with Cassandra.

'Jonathan Cross,' Mr Marlo called next, looking at his clipboard.

'It's MJ,' a pale, blond-haired boy wearing a fedora hat muttered.

'MJ?' Mr Marlo said.

'Yeah.' The boy got to his feet and walked over to Mr Marlo.

'MJ short for Jonathan Cross?' Mr Marlo said with a grin.

'No. Michael Jackson.'

A ripple of laughter passed across the studio.

The boy frowned. Billie had noticed him during the dance. It was impossible not to notice him, his ballet was exquisite. But now he seemed like a different person. Twitchy and nervous, his eyes darting all around.

'So, MJ, what do you love about dance?'

'I don't know. I suppose I love that I don't need to – to speak when I dance. I – I can speak through my body.'

'Amen to that, brother,' Mr Marlo said. 'And do you have three adjectives that best describe you?'

MJ looked at him blankly. 'I don't really . . . Dancer. Male. Autistic.'

'Thanks, MJ,' Mr Marlo said softly. 'Go take a seat.'

As Billie watched MJ go and sit down by Cassandra she felt filled with admiration. One of the regulars in her mum's cafe had autism. Her mum had explained to her how hard he found social situations. It must have been so difficult for MJ to stand up there and speak in front of them all.

'Rafael Garcia,' Mr Marlo called.

Billie almost gasped out loud as the boy with the black beads got up. She'd heard of Rafael Garcia. *DANCE* magazine had done a huge profile piece on him. He was some kind of child prodigy, supposed to be the next Mikhail Baryshnikov. Like MJ, he looked unimpressed to be there. Billie felt butterflies in her stomach as she thought of having to dance in front of him. What if she made a fool of herself? What if she fell over? She took a deep breath. *Don't worry about him*, she told herself. *Just focus on you and being your best.*

'I am Rafael Garcia,' he said in a thick Cuban

accent. 'I love to dance because dance is where I come alive.'

Billie wasn't sure if it was because he wasn't speaking in his first language but he didn't seem like he quite meant it.

'And your three adjectives?' Mr Marlo asked.

Rafael shrugged. 'Tired. Jet-lagged . . . Bored.'

Billie froze. How could he talk to Mr Marlo like that? Didn't he realize how prestigious WEDA was?

'Hmm, well we'll have to make sure we put you through your paces in the next part of the audition to make sure you don't get bored again. Sit.' Mr Marlo was clearly annoyed.

As the next few auditionees were called up, Billie felt increasingly nervous. What should she say when it was her turn? Everyone else seemed so polished, like they had been practising for days. The more Billie tried to find the right words, the more they wriggled from her grasp. And then, finally, her name was called. Somehow she made it to the front of the studio, her skin burning from the lights and the stares.

'I–I'm Billie Edmonds,' she stammered.

'And give us three adjectives that describe you, Billie,' Mr Marlo said.

'Three adjectives that describe me are . . .' Billie said, desperately trying to buy some more time. Why couldn't she think of anything? But then she pictured her mum and dad and Uncle Charlie standing at the back of the studio. *Tell them who you are, Billerina*, she imagined Charlie saying.

'I'm a dancer and a dreamer and a doer.'

'A doer?' Mr Marlo echoed.

'Yes. I don't just dream of things – I try to make them happen, no matter what.'

'Yes, I can see that,' Mr Marlo said, looking at her dust-streaked bare feet. 'And why do you love to dance?'

Just tell him the truth, Billie imagined her dad whispering to her.

'Really, I should hate dancing,' she said.

People stopped fidgeting and the studio became completely silent.

'Oh. Why's that?' Mr Marlo asked, looking surprised.

'The only reason I started going to ballet classes was because my dad died. My mum thought it would be a distraction for me – to stop me feeling so sad.' Billie looked at Mr Marlo uncertainly and he nodded at her to continue. 'But after a while my ballet classes went from being somewhere I went to take my mind off my dad to somewhere I went just to be myself. That's the only way I can describe it. When I dance I'm totally . . . me. And I don't care about any of the things that usually stress me out – like how I look, or whether people like me . . . or even if I have the right shoes.'

Mr Marlo laughed.

'So, I love dancing because dancing helps me be me.'

'Bravo!' Mr Marlo said. 'Thank you, Billie. Go take a seat.'

After everyone had spoken, they were split into groups of five to practise together before dancing for a panel of judges. Billie's heart sank as she was put in a group with Cassandra.

'Nice try with the sob story,' Cassandra whispered as they went into a smaller studio to practise. 'But this is what really counts – the dancing.'

As Billie watched Cassandra march over to the barre her skin prickled with anger. She hadn't talked about her dad dying to get sympathy. She'd said it because it was true. Well, she'd show Cassandra.

After a whirlwind hour of practice it was time to go back to the main studio to dance for the judges. As they entered the room Billie's hands felt clammy and her mouth went dry. Would Miss Murphy be there?

But the panel was made up of Mr Marlo and two women who she didn't recognize. Billie didn't know whether to be relieved or disappointed.

In the group dance Cassandra went out of her way to steal the spotlight, constantly pushing her way to the front and blocking Billie. Billie knew she hadn't done enough in the group dance to shine, so it was all resting on her solo.

As Billie stood there, waiting for the music for her solo audition to start, she thought of her dad. She thought of all the people he'd helped in his short life. She thought of how much she and her mum loved him; how devastated they'd been when he'd died. She pictured that love and sorrow drifting into her as the music started and then she began to dance. It was as if her body was telling the story of her loss. Every move was fuelled by a bitter-sweet mixture of pain and love. By the time the music faded Billie had completely forgotten where she was, she was so lost in the dance. She fell to her knees and closed her eyes.

'That was beautiful,' one of the women judges said.

'You were telling quite a story there,' Mr Marlo said gently.

Billie nodded, unable to speak.

'Thank you,' the other judge said. 'You may go now.'

As Billie made her way back through the glass walkway and then the maze of corridors in the old building, she stopped to take a look at some of the framed photos on the wall. She'd been too nervous to notice them before. But now the audition was almost over. The dancing was done, all that was left was the interview.

Most of the photos were of Miss Murphy, back in the days when she was principal dancer for the American Ballet Theatre. At the end of the corridor there was a glass case containing a pair of well-worn ballet shoes. Billie stared at them, mesmerized. They were Miss Murphy's shoes from her first role as principal dancer, in a production of *Swan Lake*. Her infamous motto '*Never say "I can't"*' was engraved on the glass.

'But what if you're not good enough?' Billie whispered.

'You should never tell yourself you're not good

enough,' a woman's voice said behind her. It was velvety and smooth, with an American accent.

Billie spun around. 'Miss Murphy!' she gasped.

'And you are?' Miss Murphy asked.

'Billie. Billie Edmonds.'

'My favourite singer was called Billie,' Miss Murphy said with a smile. She was a lot smaller than she appeared in magazines and on TV, and her bronde hair was pulled back into a bun. 'Billie Holiday. But if she'd questioned whether she was good enough she'd never have recorded a song.'

Billie nodded, speechless.

'When I was your age, auditioning to go to WEDA, I was scared to death of letting someone down. It took me a long time to realize that you can't let anyone down if you're doing your best. Our motto here is "Never say 'I can't'" because you are the only one who can unlock your potential; we can only help by giving you the tools to achieve it. Do you understand?'

Billie nodded.

'So if I were you, I'd keep believing. You never know where life might take you if you keep trying and doing your best.'

'Th-thank you,' Billie stammered.

'Goodbye, Billie,' Miss Murphy said, turning and walking away. 'And good luck in your interview.'

Billie watched as Miss Murphy strode off down the corridor, her back ruler-straight and her feet slightly turned out from years of ballet.

Had that really just happened? Had she really just spoken to Miss Murphy? She looked back at the glass case, at the words engraved into the glass. 'Never say "I can't",' Billie whispered, before heading off along the corridor.

CHAPTER
FOUR

'Are the plates ready, Billie?' Billie's mum called from the front of the cafe.

'Coming, Mum.' Billie carefully unloaded a stack of clean plates from the dishwasher and took them through to her. The lunchtime rush had just begun, the tables filling with the usual mix of workers from the nearby industrial estate and mums with their toddlers.

Her mum was wearing her normal cafe 'uniform' of jeans, T-shirt and black apron with her hair pulled back into a ponytail. 'Any news, love?' she asked, adding a sprig of watercress to a cheese sandwich.

'No.' Billie sighed. Today was the day WEDA were letting people know if they'd passed their audition. She fished her phone from her apron pocket. No new notifications. She went back into the kitchen and headed over to the sink. There was no point getting her hopes up. In the two months that had passed since the audition, she'd become convinced she hadn't got in. The only things she could seem to remember were the things that had gone wrong. Having no shoes, the way Cassandra had outshone her in the group dance, Miss Murphy overhearing her saying, 'What if you're not good enough?' Billie's face still burned at the memory.

She started rinsing the last of the dirty breakfast plates. Out in the cafe she heard her mum humming the tune to 'Somewhere Over the Rainbow'. Billie wished *she* were somewhere over the rainbow, in that place where dreams really did come true, instead of scraping congealed egg off plates. She felt her phone vibrate in her pocket and her heart dropped into the pit of her stomach.

It's probably not them, she told herself as she dried her hands.

But it *was* a message from WEDA. The title of the email was: *Your recent audition.*

Billie stared down at the screen. The second she opened the email she would know her future for sure – and the grain of hope she'd been clinging to would be gone. Her hands started trembling. She couldn't open this on her own. She headed back into the cafe.

'Mum . . .'

Her mum turned and looked at her. 'Yes, love . . . Oh my God, have you heard?'

Billie nodded.

'What did they say?'

'I don't know. I haven't opened it yet.'

Her mum placed her hands on Billie's shoulders. 'Do you want me to do it?'

'No, I'll do it. I just need you to be here.'

'Of course.'

'Any chance of a refill?' Tony, one of the cafe regulars called from the other side of the counter, holding out his empty tea mug.

'In a minute, Tony!' Billie's mum said, not moving her gaze from Billie. 'Billie's just heard from the dance academy. Go on, love, open it.'

'Blimey, this is better than watching *Britain's Got Talent*,' Tony said with a chuckle.

Billie opened the email and squinted at the screen, barely able to look. *Please, please, please*, she thought as she scanned the words.

Delighted to inform . . . offer you a place . . . start date . . . swam before her eyes.

Billie gasped.

'Have you got in?' her mum said, shakily.

Billie nodded, unable to speak.

'You have?' She grabbed Billie in a hug. 'Oh, sweetheart, I'm so proud of you. I knew you could do it. I knew it!

'She got in!' she called to the entire cafe. 'She got in!'

'Brilliant!' Tony exclaimed and all the other regulars started to cheer.

Billie leaned against the counter, unable to stop

grinning as she tried to take it all in. She read the email again, just to check she hadn't been dreaming or had misread anything. But it was all there in black and white. She had passed her audition. She had a place at WEDA – one of the top dance academies in the world.

Her mum rooted around beneath the counter and pulled out a silver gift bag. 'Congratulations, Billie,' she said, handing it to her.

'But – how did you know I was going to get in?'

'I always knew you'd do it,' her mum said, beaming with pride.

Billie fumbled through the ivory tissue paper inside and pulled out a beautiful pair of brand new ballet shoes in pale rose-pink leather. 'Mum! How did you afford these?'

'I've been saving up my tips for months,' her mum said.

'Yeah, and who's your number-one tipper?' Tony said with a grin.

'That would be you, Tony,' she replied.

'Thank you!' Billie said, grinning at him.

'No problem. Now, any chance of a cuppa, or is your number-one tipper going to die of thirst?'

'I'll get you your cuppa,' Billie's mum said, laughing.

As Billie turned the ballet shoes over in her hands, stroking the satin ribbons, she couldn't remember ever feeling happier. It was as if she'd stepped out of the cafe and over the rainbow, into that magical place where dreams really did come true.

CHAPTER
FIVE

Six weeks later, as Billie made her way up WEDA's winding driveway on the first day of term, she felt more nervous than she'd done on the day of the audition. She was now a WEDA student and she had the bag full of dance gear to prove it. All August, she and her mum had worked extra shifts at the cafe and held bake sales on their estate to raise the money for all the things she needed. As well as her brand new shoes, her bag was packed with two black leotards, a pair of pink tights, some toe pads and Band-Aids, tape and a water bottle. Most of the other students were boarders, but there was no way her mum could afford the fees, so Billie was a day student. She didn't mind the two-hour journey though – it was worth every minute to be able to attend WEDA.

The reception area was buzzing with activity when Billie walked in – making her suddenly feel very small. She gripped her bag tightly and went over to the desk.

'Hello, I'm here for the . . . the first day of term. I . . . I just started here. I'm Billie. Billie Edmonds.'

The receptionist smiled at her. 'Welcome to WEDA, Billie. Follow the signs to the main hall for the introductory talk.'

Billie heard the hall long before she could see it. It buzzed with the high-pitched, nervous chatter of the new students. She walked through the doors and looked around, wondering where she should sit.

'Hey, Billie.'

She turned and to her surprise saw Andre sitting in the back row. 'Come here,' he said, beckoning her over.

'But – wh-what . . .' Billie stammered.

'What am I doing here?' Andre said with a grin.

He looked even more striking than before, dressed in shiny black sweatpants and a hot pink hoodie. A lightning bolt was shaved into the side of his head.

'Yes. I mean . . . I thought – when I saw you cleaning – I didn't realize you were a student here . . .' Billie spluttered.

Andre smiled. 'Yep, 'fraid so. Miss M's a hard taskmaster. She makes me work for my keep.'

Billie sat down beside him. Andre must be on some kind of scholarship. He must have to clean to help pay his fees.

'Yo, MJ!' Andre called, as Jonathan walked in.

'MJ shares a dorm room with me,' Andre explained. 'I've made it my mission to turn him into a social butterfly.'

He turned to MJ as he hovered beside them, his eyes looking everywhere but at them.

'MJ, this is Billie,' Andre said. 'Billie, this is my main man, MJ.'

MJ sat down next to Billie, staring straight ahead of him. 'Hello,' he muttered.

'It's a work in progress,' Andre whispered.

Billie felt someone tap her on the shoulder.

'Hey, nearly-namesake.'

She turned to see Tilly sitting down in the seat directly behind her. Tilly's hair was now bubble-gum pink and her eyes were heavily lined in black, making them look particularly cat-like.

'So, are you going to introduce us?' Andre said, looking at Billie.

'Sorry. This is Tilly. Tilly, this is Andre and MJ.'

Billie felt a warm wave of relief. It felt good to be sitting with people who knew her name, even if they were a little on the scary side. But then her heart sank as Cassandra swept into the room.

'Uh-oh, here comes the ice queen,' Tilly muttered.

Billie watched as Cassandra made her way up the hall, then abruptly came to a halt . . . right by Rafael. Rafael Garcia – DANCE magazine's ballet prodigy – was at WEDA! Billie watched as Cassandra said something to him, and Rafael moved to let her sit down. Then Rafael said something to Cassandra and she flung her head back and laughed artificially loud, flicking her shiny brown hair over her shoulders.

The hall fell silent as an elegant older woman wearing a long black dress went up on to the stage. Her white hair was cut into a shoulder-length bob.

'Welcome to WEDA, everyone,' she said briskly. 'My name's Mrs Jones and I am the headmistress here.'

Billie looked at her in awe. Mrs Jones had been Miss Murphy's teacher back when she was a student at WEDA. Miss Murphy was always talking about how grateful she was to her in interviews.

'Here at WEDA we have very high standards,' Mrs Jones continued. 'Standards that we expect you to maintain at all times. The reason we are one of the most well-respected dance academies in the world is because we hold fast to our traditions. These traditions are incredibly important, because they keep us in tune with the history of dance and all those who have gone before us. And speaking of someone who has gone before you . . .' she smiled towards the back of the hall, 'I'm delighted to welcome our Head of Dance and Wellness, Miss Murphy, to the stage.'

Everyone started clapping as Miss Murphy walked gracefully up the aisle. She was wearing a black, pinstriped shift dress and red high-heeled shoes, and her hair was scraped back into a bun. A hush fell as Miss Murphy went up on to the stage. She smiled and clasped her hands together.

'Welcome, students, to the most prestigious dance school in the world. I am Miss Murphy, the Head of Dance and Wellness at the academy. Here at WEDA we expect you to never say "I can't" and to always do your very best. The hard truth of the dance world is, no matter how good you think you are, there is always someone, somewhere, who is better. We are here to help you work hard and push you to be your best. If you ever doubt yourself, just remember that we have chosen you because we believe in you. But it's up to you to work hard, dream big and believe in yourself.' She paused and looked around the hall, smiling as her gaze rested for a moment on Billie. 'I owe a lot of my success to my positive attitude and determination. I'm a very strong, focused woman and I'm here to encourage you to find those traits within yourself,' Miss Murphy looked at Rafael, 'and to do the work required to help you believe in your dreams and achieve them. I'm so looking forward to getting to know you, challenging you, and celebrating your mini dance victories along the way!'

Miss Murphy walked over to the edge of the stage. 'I help to run WEDA like one big family. I am adamant that we support each other, cheer each other on, and show the world just how dignified we are as artists. I want you to dive into a journey of self-discovery and show me who you are as dancers. And if I had to give you just one piece of advice, I would tell you to remember that intention – that is, the feeling and emotion behind your dance – and storytelling are everything when it comes to the perfect performance. One other thing you should all be aware of – after-hours dance activities are allowed, but we have two rules: don't let them interfere with your work at WEDA, and no extra-curricular dancing before a WEDA competition or show. At those times we need all your focus. If you break one of these rules there will be serious consequences – isn't that right, Mr Marlo?' She looked over at Mr Marlo, who was standing at the side of the stage.

'That's right, Miss M!' Mr Marlo said with a grin.

'I was once in your position,' Miss Murphy said. 'Sitting here, in this very hall, as a new student to WEDA. I know how nervous you're feeling. I know how badly you want this. And I'm living proof of what can happen if you grab all of the opportunities you'll be given here and work hard. Congratulations, students, you've made it to WEDA – but now the hard work really begins! I'll hand you over to Mr Marlo, who will fill you in on the more practical matters. Thank you, everyone, and welcome.'

As Miss Murphy made her way down from the stage, the hall filled with applause. Billie's hands stung from clapping so hard and her whole body buzzed with excitement.

'Cool,' Mr Marlo said, taking to the stage. 'Now to get down to business. In a moment, you'll all be given your weekly timetable. This will be made up of a mixture of dance and academic subjects.'

Billie heard Tilly groan behind her.

'All of you will be doing two hours of ballet per week, plus you'll get to choose two new styles of dance each term. Here at WEDA we offer a huge range of dance so there's everything from bhangra to Irish dancing.'

Andre muttered something under his breath but Billie didn't catch what he said.

'I also have some exciting news,' Mr Marlo said. 'At the end of term, some of you will be performing in a showcase at an awesome venue – the Royal Albert Hall.'

A ripple of excitement spread through the

hall and a shiver ran up Billie's spine.

'Not all of you can take part,' Mr Marlo continued. 'So it will be an opportunity for you to experience the realities of practising and auditioning for a big show. And it'll give you all a huge incentive to raise your game. OK, go sign up for your dance classes at the back of the hall, then we'll reconvene in the Murphy Wing for my special Welcome to WEDA West African dance session. That'll bring out the dance warriors in you!'

Billie had already decided which classes she wanted to take, so she headed straight over to the modern and bhangra tables. To her dismay she saw Cassandra signing up for the same.

Billie looked down at the handouts she'd been given and her face fell. She'd only just realized that need new dancewear for each class.

'What's wrong with you?' Cassandra said.

Billie shrugged. 'Nothing.'

Cassandra moved closer. 'You know you really shouldn't be here if you can't afford it – you're just wasting everyone's time.' She turned on her heel and headed to the door, leaving Billie staring after her, her face burning.

CHAPTER
SIX

When Billie had dreamed of becoming a student at WEDA, she'd imagined herself beginning every day with a smile on her face and a spring in her step. But, as she made her way up the winding driveway the next morning, not even the tweeting of the birds or the green patchwork of fields could cheer her up. How was she going to pay for her extra dance gear? When she'd got home last night her mum had looked so pale and tired she hadn't dared tell her. And anyway, her mum had already spent every last spare penny she had on Billie's dancing, she couldn't ask her for any more – it would only add to her stress. But who *could* she ask?

As she got closer to the academy, she saw Andre

hurrying round the side of the building. He was wearing a beanie hat and his hoodie pulled up but she could tell it was him from the way he walked – like he was sashaying along a catwalk. The bright lime green leggings and purple high-tops gave her a clue, too.

'Andre,' she called.

Andre stopped and for a moment he looked really guilty, like he'd been caught committing some kind of crime. Then a relieved smile of recognition spread across his face.

'Billie! Here nice and early again, I see.'

Billie laughed. Then she had a brainwave. 'Can I ask you something?'

'Depends. If it's "how do you look so effortlessly fabulous first thing in the morning, Andre?", then fire away. If it's something deadly dull like "do you know if it's going to rain later?" then I'm afraid you're wasting your time.'

Billie laughed again. 'Actually, it's neither. I was just wondering about your cleaning.'

'My cleaning?'

'Yes, you know, on the day of the auditions, when you were mopping the floor.'

'Ah, yes.' Andre nodded.

'Do you know if they need any other cleaners here?'

Andre looked at her and raised his perfectly plucked eyebrows. 'Why?'

'I . . . I need to earn some extra money.'

'Why?'

'It's . . .' Billie looked away, embarrassed. 'It's to pay for my dance kit. I didn't realize we'd need so much stuff.' She glanced back at Andre, worried that he'd be looking at her like Cassandra had, like she didn't belong. But he was nodding like he really understood.

'Sure, let's go ask.'

'What, now?'

'No time like the present!' Andre said, setting off towards the main building. 'Who invented that saying anyway? Personally, I think there's no time like the future.'

'Why?' Billie ran to keep up with him.

'Because in the future I'll be freeeee!'

Billie followed him into the reception. What did he mean, in the future he'd be free? From what? Didn't he like being at WEDA? Andre led her along a corridor and up a flight of stairs. They emerged into a shorter corridor at the top of the old building. The wood-panelled walls were lined with plaques – all the different awards WEDA had won over the years. Then Billie saw something that almost made her heart stop – a gold sign on one of the doors saying *Mrs Jones – Headmistress*. Surely he wasn't taking her to see Mrs Jones?

'Where are you taking me?' Billie whispered.

'Chill, I'm not taking you to see *her*,' Andre said, leading her past Mrs Jones's office. He came to a halt outside the next door. The sign said *Miss Murphy – Head of Dance and Wellness*.

'Miss Murphy?' Billie gasped. 'But isn't there someone else we can see? Someone less important?'

'Huh!' Andre muttered and then to her horror,

he marched straight in without even knocking.

Billie stood rooted to the spot.

'Come on!' Andre said, reappearing from the office and grabbing Billie's hand. He pulled her in after him.

Miss Murphy was sitting behind a huge mahogany desk in front of a window, typing on her laptop. 'Yes?' she said, without looking up.

Billie frowned. She would never have guessed Miss Murphy would be so laidback about having her office invaded.

'This is Billie,' Andre said, before going and sitting on the edge of Miss Murphy's desk.

Billie's mouth gaped open in shock. What was he doing? Was he trying to get them expelled before the first term had even begun?

'Ah yes, we already met.' Miss Murphy looked over her glasses at Billie and smiled. 'And to what do I owe the pleasure of this early morning visit?'

'She needs a job,' Andre said.

Billie cringed. Why was he being so informal?

Didn't he know who Miss Murphy was? Had he somehow managed to miss all the press coverage about her career?

'A job?' Miss Murphy echoed. She took off her glasses. 'What kind of job?'

'A cleaning job – to pay for her dance gear.'

Then, to Billie's horror, Andre started doing dramatic leg stretches on Miss Murphy's desk. She waited for her to start yelling – to tell them both to get out and never come back again – but to her surprise, Miss Murphy went over to Andre and corrected his pose. 'Hold your core and straighten your spine,' she said. Then she turned to Billie. 'You're on a day scholarship, right?'

Billie nodded. 'I didn't realize how much stuff I'd need. My mum . . . We don't have very much money.'

Miss Murphy nodded. Andre started pirouetting dangerously close to a lamp.

'Andre, what have I told you about practising next to the light-fittings?'

'Sorry, Mum,' Andre muttered.

'*Mum?*' Billie stared from Andre to Miss Murphy and back again.

''Fraid so,' Andre said with a grin.

'But . . .'

'What? You can't figure out how I got my stunning good looks?'

'Andre!' Miss Murphy scolded, but she was smiling.

'I thought . . .' Billie was still speechless. 'You were cleaning the hall on the day of the auditions. I thought you were on a scholarship.'

'Yeah, she makes me do it.' Andre nodded towards Miss Murphy. 'For the same reason she never talks about me in interviews and keeps me out of the limelight. Says she wants to keep me humble. Not that it'll ever work. I'm way too fabulous to be humble.'

Miss Murphy laughed and shook her head before looking back at Billie. 'What dance gear do you still need to buy, Billie?'

'Outfits for my modern and bhangra classes.'

'OK. Well, how about I give you the money to buy it today and you can pay the academy back by cleaning one of the studios after school every other day, for this term?'

Billie was overcome with relief. She was going to get her dance gear. She was going to be able to stay at the academy!

'Thank you,' she gasped.

'Can I be her personal shopper?'

'Oh I don't know, Andre, I think that's up to Billie,' Miss Murphy said, going back behind her desk.

'Seriously, let me come with you,' Andre said. 'I can take you to the hottest place in London. You'll have major swag once I'm finished with you. We can go after school.'

'OK,' Billie said. It would definitely be fun to go shopping with Andre.

'Right, don't you two have lessons to go to?' Miss Murphy said, putting her glasses back on.

'Come and see me at the end of the day, Billie, and I'll have the money ready for you.'

Billie smiled at her gratefully. 'Thank you so, so much.'

'Just think of me as the style whisperer,' Andre said to Billie as they got off the train in London later that afternoon. 'I can get anyone's threads under control – even yours,' he said with a grin.

Billie laughed as she followed him through the ticket barrier. She really liked Andre – even when he teased her it was done in fun – unlike Cassandra. Billie shuddered as she thought back on her first day of classes at WEDA. Cassandra had taken centre stage in every one of them, looking down scornfully on everyone else – apart from Rafael. Still, that didn't matter now. Now it was just her and Andre – and about half of the world by the looks of it. Leicester Square was swarming with a mixture of camera-wielding tourists, foreign students and commuters. A woman walked past them wearing sky-high platform boots and a shiny silver hat.

'OMG! I have to get her picture!' Andre exclaimed, taking his phone from his pocket.

Billie watched as he ran after the woman. Andre said something to her and she burst out laughing, and the next thing Billie knew Andre had the woman leaning against a lamppost posing for a picture. Billie watched as Andre fished a business card from his pocket and handed it to the woman. Then he hugged her like they were old friends and returned to Billie.

'Sorry about that. I can never ignore a UPO,' he said.

'UPO?' Billie looked at him questioningly.

'Urgent Photo Opp,' he explained, although nothing was really any clearer to Billie.

'I have a fashion blog,' Andre said as they started heading up towards Soho. 'It's called Spotted. I post pictures of cool outfits I spot when I'm out and about. Maybe one day I'll feature you – once you've unleashed your IF.'

'IF?'

'Inner Fashionista,' Andre said with a grin. 'Everyone's got one, it's just that not everyone knows where to find it. But don't worry, that's where *I* come in.'

Billie followed Andre down a narrow, cobbled side-street.

'This place is uh-may-zing,' he said, leading her into a shop called The Crooked Tutu. 'It's where all the serious dancers go.'

The shop was cool and dark and smelled of patchouli oil. An old jazz song was playing softly through speakers in the ceiling.

'Andre!' the woman behind the counter exclaimed. 'How are you, darling? How's your mum?' The woman's long silver hair was pinned up on to her head in a bun. Although she was about sixty, Billie could tell she'd once been a dancer. She still had the upright ballet poise.

'We're fabulous, Gloria,' Andre replied. 'This is my friend Billie. We're here to give her a makeover.'

'You go for it,' Gloria said. 'I'm right here if you need me for anything.'

The next twenty minutes were a kaleidoscope of colour, as Andre led Billie around the store, holding up leotards, skirts and wraparound tops. Each time, he would either frown or grin. All the outfits that got a grin were slung into the netting basket Billie was carrying. The frowns were placed straight back on the hanger. Finally, they'd searched every rack and Billie had a basketful.

'Now for the moment of truth,' Andre said, leading Billie to the dressing room. 'You are about to reveal your true self, Billie Edmonds. Are you ready?'

'Oh, but . . .' Billie stood in the doorway. Was he going to come in with her and watch her undress?

'Oh darling, don't look so scared. You're not my type.'

Billie frowned.

Andre laughed. 'Don't take it personally. Your

entire gender is not my type. Look, if it makes you feel better, I'll wait outside the cubicle and you can come show me when you're ready.'

Billie went into the cubicle and pulled the curtain. The riot of colour in the basket was a long way from her normal palette of pale pink, grey and black. She slipped out of her sweatshirt and put on a vivid purple leotard.

'You ready yet?' Andre called from the other side of the curtain.

Billie pulled back the curtain.

'Hmm.' Andre pursed his lips and looked her up and down. 'Try it back to front.'

'What?'

'The leotard. Put it on back to front. Over the orange crop top.'

'OK . . .' Billie did as she was told and looked in the mirror. To her surprise, it actually looked good.

'Can I see?' Andre said, poking his head round the curtain. 'Boom shakalaka! Now try the hot peach wraparound with the stripy leggings.'

Once again, he was right. The combination looked great!

'How do you know?' Billie asked, admiring her reflection in the changing-room mirror.

'Know what?'

'What will go together.'

'I told you, I'm the style whisperer.' Andre started adjusting the spikes of his hair in the mirror. 'Seriously though, so much of fashion is just daring to be different – with the emphasis on daring.'

'What do you mean?'

'It's all about the swagger.' Andre turned back to look at her. 'Pull your shoulders back.'

Billie did as she was told.

'Now hold your head up high. See how much better you look. Confidence is everything!'

Billie nodded.

'You just have to be proud of you.'

Billie smiled. Although they looked very different, there was no doubting he was Miss Murphy's son.

After they'd paid for Billie's new dance gear they

bought giant ice-creams and sat people-watching in Leicester Square.

'So, is ballet your passion, like it is your mum's?' Billie asked.

Andre shook his head. 'No, my passion's street dance.'

'Street dance?' Billie frowned. 'But that isn't on the syllabus at WEDA.'

'Tell me about it.' Andre sighed. 'I've tried everything I can to get my mum to change her mind – I even went on a hunger strike.'

Billie stared at him.

'She got me to crack after two hours. She bought me a red velvet cupcake. That woman knows all my weak spots. She can be truly evil sometimes.'

'Why won't she have street dance on the syllabus?'

'She doesn't think it's a *proper* form of dance.' Andre sighed again. 'But I don't care. I figured out a way round it.'

'What do you mean?'

'I'm setting up a street crew at WEDA – in secret.

I've hand-picked a few dancers I think will be up for it and won't blab.' He turned to Billie. 'And I'd like you to be one of them.'

CHAPTER
SEVEN

The next morning's lessons were all academic. Maths, followed by Science and then French. Cassandra, who had been typically smug in Maths and Science, started majorly showing off in French.

'What's the French for "annoying pig"?' Tilly muttered to Billie as Cassandra started talking to the teacher in fluent French.

'Le pig annoyiiiiing?' Billie said and Tilly started to laugh. It was the first time Billie had seen her smile all morning. Tilly clearly didn't enjoy the academic subjects nearly as much as she liked to dance.

'I just don't get why we need to speak another language,' Tilly said. 'We're here to learn to dance.'

'Is there a problem, Tilly?' the teacher said, looking at her sternly.

'No, Madame Hermet,' Tilly said sullenly.

'Good. Now let's conjugate some verbs.'

'Whoop-de-doop,' Tilly muttered.

When the bell finally rang for lunch Billie's heart skipped a beat. It was time for Andre's street crew audition.

'I – uh – I can't come to the canteen with you today,' Tilly said. 'I have to do some extra Maths work.'

'Good – I mean – OK. I'll see you in ballet after.' Billie stood up feeling really relieved. At least she didn't have to lie to Tilly about what she was doing for lunch now, though she felt bad about not telling her what she was up to. She left the classroom and went to shove her bag in her locker. Then she made her way out of the main building and round to a pathway that led to a copse of trees. According to Andre, there was an old stable way out through the trees that never got used, so he'd claimed it for his secret street dance HQ. Billie followed the pathway, and there at the foot of the hill was an old ramshackle stable. Billie paused outside the door. What if she'd come to the wrong place? Or even worse, what if it was a prank? Or a test, to see whether she'd obey the rules at WEDA? What if Miss Murphy had put Andre up to it?

'Are you coming in or not?' Andre peered out of the door and pulled her inside.

Billie blinked, trying to adjust her eyes to the gloom.

'Excuse the décor,' Andre said, following her gaze around the stable. 'My interior design team haven't had a chance to work their magic yet. I'm calling the current look "Rustic Charm Chic".'

Billie saw a couple of other people at the far side of the stable. MJ was pacing up and down by the far wall and – Billie let out a surprised laugh – Tilly was sitting cross-legged in the corner, writing something in a notebook.

'Tilly!' she cried, walking over.

Tilly's face lit up. 'He invited you too! I couldn't say where I was going earlier cos Andre was being all top secret about it. I'm so glad you're here.'

Billie shrugged. 'Yeah well, I don't know if I'm going to be good enough – I've never tried street dance before.'

'You'll be great,' Tilly said.

'What time are we starting?' MJ looked at his watch anxiously.

'We're just waiting for one more person,' Andre said.

Billie had a moment of panic – what if that one more person was Cassandra?

'Ah, here he is,' Andre said, opening the stable door.

Billie felt a weird mixture of relief and excitement as Rafael walked in.

'Hey,' he muttered to Andre.

'Hey,' Andre replied. 'OK, we haven't got long so let's get started. I invited you all here today because you've expressed an interest in street dance which, as we know, is a crime worse than drowning cute puppies here at WEDA. So we need to keep this on the down-low.' He looked around the group solemnly. 'No one must speak a word of what goes on here, all right?'

The others nodded. Billie's stomach lurched. What if they got caught? She wasn't even sure she wanted to street dance. It would be just her luck to get into trouble for something she didn't really want to do.

Andre went over to an iPod deck perched on top of an old storage crate. 'Why don't we freestyle for a while – see what happens?'

'Yes!' Tilly exclaimed, leaping to her feet. 'I'm so ready to dance after a morning sat at a desk.'

Andre pressed play and the beats of a hip-hop track filled the stable. Billie watched as Andre and Tilly started freestyling together. Then MJ joined in, tipping his hat down low over his face. Billie felt a wave of panic. There was no way she could pull off the kind of acrobatic moves they were doing – she was a ballerina. She found it very hard to let go of her posture and move the way street dancers did. But what about Rafael? He was a ballet prodigy, surely this wouldn't be his kind of thing either? But then Rafael started nodding his head in time to the beat and he danced his way over to the others.

Andre whooped and made room for him. Billie stood watching Rafael, mesmerized. His toned body, which had been so taut and poised in the ballet audition, was now contorting into all kinds of shapes. She was torn between wanting to run from the stable and standing there spellbound.

'Come on, Billie,' Tilly said, dancing over to her.

Billie felt horrible. She was so used to following choreography that being left to her own devices felt terrifying – especially in front of dancers as accomplished as these. It was like the first time you try riding a bike without stabilizers – and she had the dreadful feeling she wasn't nearly ready.

'I don't know if –'

'Come on.' Tilly grabbed her hand and pulled her into the group.

Instinctively, Billie began copying Andre, as if he were the choreographer. But then Andre began rolling his body like his spine was made of rubber. How did he do that? Billie tried to make hers do the same but her body felt so stiff. It was like her core was made of steel. MJ did a flawless moonwalk across the floor and the others started whooping.

'That was *beat!*' Tilly cried. She danced into the centre of the floor and started dancing as if her entire body was a wave in the ocean.

Rafael started sliding from left to right. Then suddenly he collapsed to the floor and started spinning on his hands with his legs flaring out, faster and faster until he was a blur.

Andre whooped and then he took centre circle, doing an old-style running man. Then he slowed it right down, like a real-life slow-motion replay. Again Billie was mesmerized. Andre looked at her and gestured at her to take the centre. The others all clapped along in time, watching and waiting. Billie's face flushed and her heart pounded. What should she do? She did a few big fan kicks into turning leaps across the floor. She tried letting her body go to the music but she instinctively ended up going on her toes and doing some weird ballet moves. She stopped dancing and stood still. 'I'm sorry, I-I don't think I can do this,' she stammered. 'Could I just watch you guys for a bit?'

'Of course,' Andre said.

Billie sat down on the floor, feeling embarrassed and useless.

The first lesson after lunch was gymnastics with Mr Marlo.

'Today we're going to be working on aerial cartwheels,' he said as the students positioned themselves in front of their mats.

Billie tried and tried but every time she propelled herself over she instinctively put out one hand.

'Come on, you can do it,' Mr Marlo said, after her tenth attempt.

'I can't,' Billie said, sitting dejected on the mat.

'Uh-oh,' Mr Marlo said. 'What is Miss Murphy's motto?'

'Never say "I can't",' Billie muttered.

'That'll be ten press-ups please,' Mr Marlo said. 'Hopefully it will remind you to never give up on yourself.'

Mr Marlo's words were still ringing in her ears when Billie went to bed that night. It had been so amazing when he'd praised her at the audition. Messing up in front of him today and seeing the disappointment on his face had been crushing. It had been such a rubbish day. It was all very well never saying 'I can't' but what if you really couldn't? She'd tried street dancing and she'd tried an aerial cartwheel but they'd both felt impossible. Maybe Cassandra was right. Maybe Billie didn't belong at WEDA. Maybe she should give up on her dream and go back to normal school – it would certainly save her mum a lot of money and make things easier at home.

But as soon as she thought this she felt a

hollowness inside. Who would she be without her dream? What would she do? But she was so tired of the endless fight to turn the *I can'ts* into *I cans*, and stay strong for her mum. It was so draining. Then she remembered Uncle Charlie's poem and took it from her jewellery box. As she re-read his words she realized that there was no way she could quit now. Like Uncle Charlie, she was a doer as well as a dreamer. And she was going to do whatever it took to make her dream come true. Tomorrow would be a fresh new day and she'd try her hardest to do her best. Tomorrow she would say, *I can.*

CHAPTER EIGHT

Billie's first lesson the next morning was English. As she and Tilly made their way into the classroom she saw the teacher writing something on the white board. Billie felt a wave of relief as she read the word: *POETRY*. Surely this was something she *could* do.

She followed Tilly to a table right at the back.

'Hopefully the teacher won't notice me back here,' Tilly explained. But Billie very much doubted that. Tilly's hair was now bright cornflower blue.

Rafael walked into the classroom, his head bowed. He came and sat at the table next to theirs but didn't look over. Then Cassandra came in. She scanned the room, until her gaze fell on Rafael and she smiled and went and sat down next to him.

'I hate English,' Tilly muttered.

'Really?' Billie stared at her in shock. She didn't get how someone could not like English, especially poetry. Reading and writing were her favourite things after dancing. She loved the way writers could create whole new worlds with words.

'My brain doesn't like words,' Tilly said, taking her phone out of her bag. 'Have you seen Andre's fashion blog? He's asked me to help him with it. We were up half the night dying my hair for it. Look at the pictures.'

Billie felt a wistful pang. Being a day student meant she missed out on the fun that was had in the dorms in the evenings. She watched as Tilly scrolled through photos of her posing for Andre.

At the front of the class the teacher cleared her throat. 'Hello, everyone, and welcome to English. My name's Mrs Jarvis. A few house rules before we get started. No talking while I'm talking and absolutely *no phones*.' She looked pointedly at Tilly.

'Huh, so much for not being noticed,' Tilly whispered.

'Today we're going to be starting with a real treat – we're going to be reading some poems by Emily Dickinson.'

'Yippee,' Tilly muttered sarcastically.

Billie frowned. She hoped Tilly wasn't going to keep up this gloom all through the lesson.

'The first poem I'd like you to read is one called "Hope",' Mrs Jarvis continued, walking around the classroom handing out photocopied poems. 'While you're reading it I want you to underline anything you particularly like.'

Billie did what she usually did with poems – read it through fast once then re-read it again slowly, looking for treasure. This was something her Uncle Charlie had taught her to do. Apparently there were all kinds of hidden gems buried inside poems but you only found them if you looked hard enough. She liked the first two lines of this poem the best:

Hope is the thing with feathers
That perches in the soul.

Billie pictured a little bird perching inside her ribcage, giving her hope that things would all work out OK at WEDA; that she did have what it takes to succeed there. She took out her pen and underlined the first two lines. Then she glanced at Tilly. She wasn't even looking at the poem, just staring sullenly out of the window. Across from them, Cassandra whispered something in Rafael's ear. Billie sighed.

'OK, let's read the poem out loud before we discuss it.' Mrs Jarvis walked to the back of the class and her gaze rested on Tilly. 'Would you like to begin please?'

'What?' Tilly sat bolt upright.

'Could you read the first stanza to the rest of the class?'

'But . . .'

Everyone turned to look at Tilly and her face flushed bright red.

'Just the first stanza,' Mrs Jarvis said.

'What's a stanza?' Tilly asked.

'Oh my God!' Cassandra exclaimed. 'Who doesn't know what a stanza is?'

Billie glared at her.

'Shut up, Miss Know-it-all,' Tilly snapped.

'That's enough of that – read the poem please,' Mrs Jarvis said, frowning at Tilly.

'That's the first stanza,' Billie whispered, pointing to it on Tilly's poem.

Tilly sighed. Then she picked up the poem and began to read. '*Hope is the – the thing with . . .*' she broke off and frowned . . . '*fathers?*'

Cassandra let out a high-pitched laugh.

'What's your problem?' Tilly yelled at her.

'That is enough!' Mrs Jarvis said sternly. 'Tilly, see me after class please. Would anyone else like to read it?'

Cassandra's hand shot up.

'Thank you, Cassandra.'

'Hope is the thing with *feathers*,' she began,

looking at Tilly.

Tilly slumped back in her chair, looking completely hopeless.

Billie picked up her pen and scribbled a quick note to her on the foot of her poem. *Don't worry, I'll help you.* She shoved the paper across the table to Tilly. Tilly looked at her and gave a weak smile. Her eyes were shiny with tears.

'I'm dyslexic,' Tilly said as they made their way to the dance studios after class. 'It doesn't matter how hard I try, words always get jumbled up in my mind and then I get so frustrated and . . .' She broke off and sighed. 'All I want to do is dance. It's the only thing I'm any good at. I hate having to do all these other stupid lessons.'

'I can help you with your English if you like?' Billie looked at her cautiously.

'Seriously?'

'Of course.'

Tilly looked at her for a moment then she

grabbed her in a hug. 'Thank you!'

She linked arms with Billie as they continued to walk. 'Are you coming to the street dance practice at lunchtime?'

Billie shook her head. 'I don't think street dance is for me. I think I'm going to focus on my ballet and try to get into the showcase.'

'Oh.' Tilly looked so disappointed that it made Billie feel both happy and sad. Happy she seemed to have made a genuine friend. Sad that she wouldn't be able to hang out with her as part of the street crew.

After classes had finished for the day, Billie went to the caretaker's office to get her cleaning instructions. The caretaker was a friendly, twinkly-eyed man with short white hair, whose name was Ted.

'Aha, you must be my new helper,' he said as Billie peered round his office door. 'Let me get you your supplies.' Ted went into a store room and returned with a mop, bucket, polish and cloths. 'Follow me,' he said.

Ted led her to the ballet studios in the oldest part of the academy. 'Miss Murphy told me to give you this one,' he said, leading her into the Fontaine Studio. 'She gave me a note for you too. Now where did I put it?' Ted began rummaging through the pockets in his overalls. 'Ah, here it is.' He handed Billie the envelope. 'It's pretty simple really. Mop the floor and polish the mirrors. Any problems, give us a shout.'

'Will do.'

As soon as he'd gone Billie opened the envelope.

Billie,

When I first came to WEDA as a student, I too had to clean the studios to pay for my dance gear — this very studio in fact. The harder you have to work for a dream, the sweeter it is to achieve.

Miss Murphy

Billie looked round the studio. She pictured a thirteen-year-old Miss Murphy standing right where she was now, mop in hand. Surely she must have felt just as scared and nervous when she started here – even more so probably, as she was so far from home – but look at all she'd gone on to achieve. Billie felt excitement rippling through her. She *could* do this. She fished her iPod from her bag and turned it on. After Miss Murphy had told her she liked Billie Holiday, Billie had downloaded an album of her greatest hits. She selected it now. She wondered if Miss Murphy had listened to Billie Holiday when she cleaned in here too. Obviously not on an iPod, but maybe on one of those big clunky Walkman things that played old-fashioned cassette tapes. As Billie cleaned, it was as if she was getting rid of all the stress of the past couple of days – mopping and polishing it into the mirror and floor. Then finally it was done.

As Billie leaned against the barre and admired her work, one of her favourite Billie Holiday tracks came on, a song called 'All of Me'. The first time she'd heard it Billie had started to cry.

It was all about the sadness you feel after losing someone. It had made Billie think of her dad. She felt that same emotion now, coming through the ear-buds, into her brain and expanding out into her whole body. She stretched out her arms in time with the melody. Then she stepped forwards and began to dance.

By the time the song came to an end Billie felt as if her entire body was radiating sorrow. But she didn't feel sad. Dancing her feelings about her dad always felt healing, as if the pain was being transformed into something beautiful. She leaned on the barre to catch her breath and the silence of the studio was broken by the sound of someone clapping. Billie looked up and saw Andre in the mirror. He was standing by the door, still clapping.

'Girl, you betta werk!' he said, coming over to her. 'What were you listening to? Your dancing was on *point*.'

'Oh, it was nothing, I was just having a bit of a ballet freestyle,' Billie said, embarrassed.

'Why didn't you come to the street meet at lunchtime?' Andre asked, checking his eyebrows in the mirror.

'I don't think it's for me,' Billie said, gathering up her cleaning things.

'But you only tried it once.' Andre grabbed her by the hand. 'Come on, let me show you some of the basics.'

Billie followed him into the centre of the studio. At least this time there was no one else watching so it wouldn't be quite so embarrassing.

'You need to loosen up here,' Andre said, placing a hand on her stomach.

'But how?' Billie asked. 'Ballet's all about having a really tight core. I don't know how to let go.'

'Try doing a roll,' Andre said. 'Like this.' He did a roll and it was like watching a wave run up his spine.

Billie tried copying him but she looked and felt like a robot. 'I just *can't* get the hang of it,' she sighed.

'OK, that'll be two hundred press-ups,' Andre said, giving her a super stern glare.

'What?'

'You said the forbidden word!' Andre said. 'There's no such thing as "can't", remember. At least not here at WEDA.'

Billie laughed. Then she tried another roll.

'You're still way too poised,' Andre said. 'You need to find your inner swag.'

'But what if I don't have any inner swag?' Billie said, starting to feel frustrated.

'Everyone has inner swag,' Andre retorted. 'It's just that in some people it's hidden under layers and layers of uptightness.'

'I'm not uptight!' Billie exclaimed in what she realized too late was a really uptight voice.

'Oh really.' Andre came and stood behind her so that they were both facing the mirror. 'Don't worry, I'll make a street dancer of you if it kills me. Next to MJ and his conversation skills, you're my greatest project.' He gave a dramatic sigh. 'I've sure got my work cut out for me this term.'

As Billie grinned back at him in the mirror she couldn't help thinking that Andre might have bitten off way more than he could chew. As far as she was concerned, finding her inner swag would be impossible.

CHAPTER NINE

'I've made you your favourite breakfast for good luck,' Billie's mum said, placing a bowl of fruit salad on the kitchen table.

Normally Billie loved her mum's fruit salad, but today she was so nervous it felt as if a giant fist was clenching her throat, leaving her unable to swallow. It was the day of the auditions for the showcase and Billie had decided to take a risk and perform her own original routine to 'All of Me'. Andre's enthusiastic response to her dance had been really encouraging and she'd be auditioning for Miss Murphy, so hopefully she'd appreciate the song choice. But now some doubts were starting to set in.

'Mum, can I ask you something?'

'Of course.' Her mum sat down at the table and stifled a yawn. 'Sorry, love, I haven't been sleeping well recently.'

Billie looked at her, concerned. Her mum's eyes were puffy and red, like she'd been crying. 'Mum, are you OK?'

'Yes, of course. What was it you wanted to ask me?'

Billie frowned.

'Honestly, I'm fine,' her mum said.

But she didn't look fine. Maybe she was sad that Uncle Charlie had gone off on his travels again – he'd just started a construction job out in Dubai. Maybe she was missing him.

'Go on,' she said.

'If you were having a job interview and they asked you a question and you knew that your answer to that question – the truthful answer – would be a bit unusual or different, would you tell the truth or choose another answer that didn't seem so different?'

'I'm not sure I understand what you mean, sweetheart.'

'Is it better to take a risk and be your true self or try to be the same as everyone else?'

Her mum looked at her seriously. 'It's always better to be your true self. Otherwise you'll end up unhappy and full of regret. It's like when I married your dad.' She glanced up at the picture of him on the dream-board. 'Grandma and Grandad didn't want me to.'

Billie stared at her, shocked. 'Why not?'

'Oh, it wasn't that they didn't like him, they'd just have rather I married someone with a more sensible, steady job, like a doctor or an accountant.' She looked back at the board and gave a sad little laugh. 'Instead of someone who wanted to save the world.'

'Do you ever regret not marrying someone richer?'

'No! Of course not. That's what I'm trying to tell you.' Her mum nodded to the photo. 'And what your dad would tell you if he were here today. You have to follow your heart. I don't regret a single moment of my life with your dad – no matter how painfully it ended.'

Billie nodded and felt a wave of relief. She'd made the right decision choosing to follow her heart with the audition. 'Thanks, Mum.'

The first class that day was bhangra. As Billie was getting changed in the dressing room Cassandra came and sat on the bench beside her.

'How are you feeling about the showcase audition?' she asked with a smile.

Billie stared at her. Why was Cassandra being friendly? It was totally unlike her.

'OK,' she replied.

'Which piece did you choose?' Cassandra asked, stretching her long, thin legs out in front of her.

'I'm going to be doing a piece of my own,' Billie replied.

'What, that you choreographed?' Cassandra's pale blue eyes widened.

'Yes.'

'But this audition is for the opportunity to be in a major showcase.'

'I know.' Billie frowned. What was Cassandra trying to say?

'Don't you think it's a bit risky to be going off-piste when there's so much at stake? Off-piste is a skiing term by the way.'

'I know!' Billie's skin prickled with anger as she pictured Cassandra whizzing down a ski slope somewhere glamorous shouting, '*Get out of my way, I'm ballet royalty!*' 'I thought it would be good to try something different – something original,' she said.

Cassandra stared at her for a moment before switching on an obviously fake smile. 'Well you wouldn't catch me doing something like that. But then I do have a lot more experience of this kind of thing than you, I guess.' Cassandra stood up and swished her hair over her shoulder. 'Good luck,' she said as she walked out the door.

Billie sat dead still on the bench, her mind racing. Had she made a massive mistake? Was it not the done thing to go 'off-piste' at a major audition? Should she be doing an established piece? She could always do the routine they'd been working on in class. She quickly stood up and started running through the routine in between the benches.

'Is everything OK, Billie?' Cassandra said, poking her head round the door, her voice sickly sweet. 'Miss Begum told me to tell you that we're all waiting for you.'

'Sorry. Just coming,' Billie said, hurrying to the door.

When it was finally time for the audition Billie felt jittery with nerves. She stepped inside the studio and looked around. Miss Murphy was sitting on the piano seat, holding a clipboard.

'Hello, Billie,' Miss Murphy said, as she walked over. 'I'm very much looking forward to seeing you dance.'

'Thank you.' Billie had a moment's hesitation as she imagined going back to her original plan, and telling Miss Murphy that she'd choreographed a routine to a Billie Holiday song. When she'd imagined this moment before, she'd pictured Miss Murphy smiling with delight. But it was no good, Cassandra's words had planted fears like seeds in her brain. This was too big an opportunity to take a risk. She had to play it safe. Billie went and plugged her iPod into the dock and selected the track they'd been dancing to in class.

Almost as soon as it began Billie got a sinking feeling. She didn't really feel any emotional connection to this piece and her movements felt mechanical, like she was going through the motions instead of living the dance. When the music came to an end, Billie could see the disappointment all over Miss Murphy's face.

'I'm sorry, Billie, but I just wasn't feeling that. *You* weren't feeling it either, were you?'

Billie shook her head. 'I'm sorry.'

'Never mind. Maybe next time,' Miss Murphy said, writing something on her clipboard.

Billie felt a hot rush of disappointment flooding

her body. 'Thank you for the opportunity,' she mumbled, then fled from the room. Cassandra was waiting outside, doing some warm-up stretches.

'How did it go?' she asked.

'It was horrible,' Billie replied.

'Oh no!' But there was an excited gleam in Cassandra's eyes that didn't match the sympathy in her voice. 'I did tell you not to take a risk.'

'I didn't,' Billie muttered. Then she took a deep breath. There was no way she was going to give Cassandra the satisfaction of seeing her upset. 'Maybe next time will be my time,' she said, before walking off down the corridor, tears burning her eyes.

Billie was actually relieved to get to her cleaning job after classes had finished. Cleaning usually helped her get rid of frustrations, but not today. Today, the harder she polished the mirrored wall, the more frustrated she got. Why had she listened to Cassandra instead of her mum? Why hadn't she followed her heart?

'You're so stupid!' she said to herself in the mirror, before squirting polish all over her reflection. The worst thing about it all was the look of disappointment on Miss Murphy's face. She'd clearly been expecting better from Billie, and Billie had let her down. She polished until her reflection came back into view. *This isn't who I want to be*, she thought as she looked at her glum expression. *I don't want to be someone too scared to follow their heart.* A feeling of determination started growing inside of her, fierce and strong. It grew and grew until she couldn't ignore it any more. Billie marched from the studio and up the stairs. Up and up until she reached the corridor where all the staff had their offices. She marched up to Miss Murphy's office and knocked on the door.

'Come in,' Miss Murphy's voice called.

Billie's heart skipped a beat, but she gripped the door handle and opened it.

'Billie!' Miss Murphy looked surprised. 'What can I do for you?'

Billie came into the room and stood in front of her desk. 'You know how you told me to believe in myself more?'

'Yes.'

'Well, I truly believe I can do a whole lot better than I did in the audition this morning.'

Miss Murphy smiled. 'That's very good to hear but the auditions are over now and –'

'The truth is, I had a whole other routine planned for you,' Billie interrupted, 'to a song by Billie Holiday, but then at the last minute I thought maybe I'd made a mistake, and maybe we weren't supposed to use original pieces for our audition so I changed it to the routine we've been doing in class.'

Miss Murphy took off her glasses and looked at Billie. It was impossible to read her expression. 'I see.'

'I know it's too late to get a place in the showcase but I would really, really like to show you the dance I'd planned to do.'

Miss Murphy nodded.

'If you're not too busy maybe I could show it to you now in the Fontaine Studio. I just finished cleaning it.'

'OK then.' Miss Murphy stood up. 'I have to say you've got me intrigued.'

It was only when she was back in the studio that the enormity of what she'd just done hit Billie. But it was too late now – Miss Murphy was sitting on the piano stool watching her expectantly.

Billie put her iPod into the dock and flicked through until she reached 'All of Me'.

'OK – so this is it,' she said nervously, before pressing play.

As soon as the notes of the jazz piano filled the air all of the tension and regret she'd been feeling melted from Billie's body. This was her time to shine. And as soon as Billie Holiday's soulful voice began singing, Billie lost herself in the melody. As she heard the words, '*I'm no good without you*', Billie thought of her dad and, just like the day

Andre had seen her dance, Billie felt all of her pain and sorrow and love blend together and fill her limbs. At times she felt weightless as she leaped and spun through the air. It was as if her body was a paintbrush painting great brushstrokes of emotion all over the studio.

Finally, the song came to an end. Billie closed her eyes as reality began prickling its way back inside of her. She opened her eyes and glanced at Miss Murphy. Miss Murphy was staring at her, transfixed. The silence in the studio seemed to stretch on forever, then finally Miss Murphy stood up.

'I believe in you, Billie, but *you* have to believe in you to make it as a dancer, do you understand?'

Billie nodded.

'Trust in your intuition – especially when it comes to big auditions. That was absolutely beautiful. I–I . . .' Miss Murphy broke off and looked away. 'That song is very important to me,' she said softly. 'It was wonderful to see you interpret it in such a moving way. Thank you.'

Miss Murphy walked over to her. 'And congratulations. You're in the show.'

Billie stared at her. 'What? But I thought . . .'

'I don't normally give people second chances at auditions, Billie, but you earned your place with that dance.' Then she turned and was gone.

Billie looked at her shocked reflection in the mirror and burst out laughing with excitement and relief. She was in the showcase!

CHAPTER TEN

The following morning, when Billie showed up for the first rehearsal for the ballet showcase, Cassandra was unable to hide her shock.

'What? But I thought . . .' She gaped at Billie like a goldfish. 'I thought you hadn't got through the audition.'

Billie smiled at her. 'Miss Murphy changed her mind.'

'But . . .'

Billie looked around the studio. All of the other students in the showcase were warming up – apart from Rafael, who was sitting cross-legged in the corner. Billie's skin prickled with nerves. She hoped she didn't mess up in front of him again. She wished

Andre and Tilly were there too, but Andre had got into the tap showcase and Tilly was in the jazz. Still, it wouldn't matter that her friends weren't here once she began to dance. And Miss Murphy would be teaching them. But then the door opened and Mrs Jones walked in. She was wearing a flowing black dress and holding a cane. Billie watched her, transfixed. They were going to be taught by the Head of WEDA – by the same person who had taught Miss Murphy!

Cassandra went rushing over to her. 'I'm so glad you're going to be teaching us for our rehearsals, Mrs Jones,' Cassandra said so loudly the entire studio could hear. 'My dad sends his very best regards. Did you get the cheque he sent you?'

'I most certainly did, Cassandra,' Mrs Jones replied with a smile. 'Please thank him for his generosity. The board at WEDA are very grateful.'

Cassandra smiled. 'He says he can't wait to see me perform my solo in the showcase.'

Mrs Jones nodded. 'I'm sure you will make him very proud.'

Billie frowned. How did Cassandra already know she'd be performing a solo? They hadn't even had their first rehearsal yet. Was that why her dad had made a donation to WEDA? To buy his daughter a solo?!

Mrs Jones went to the front of the studio and rapped her cane on the floor. Everyone fell silent. Cassandra came and stood right in front of Billie. 'At the end of this term you will have the very great honour of representing WEDA at the Royal Albert Hall,' Mrs Jones said. 'This will be both a very great honour *and* a huge responsibility. The reputation of WEDA will be resting in your hands – or rather, in your feet. Do you understand?'

'Yes, Mrs Jones,' Cassandra replied loudly while the rest of them all murmured and nodded.

Billie's heart pounded. Representing WEDA at such a prestigious venue *was* a massive responsibility. She was determined not to let Mrs Jones and the Academy down.

'Right, let's begin with some poses.' Mrs Jones

started walking around among the students. As she passed Billie she called out, 'Plie!'

Billie pulled her spine up straight and bent her knees into a plie.

'Now arabesque!' Mrs Jones went back to the front of the studio and began studying them all.

Cassandra extended her arm until it was right in front of Billie's face causing Billie to wobble slightly as she raised her leg.

'You there, move back,' Mrs Jones called to Billie. 'Give Cassandra some space.'

Billie's face burned. Why should she move? Cassandra was the one who'd deliberately come and stood right in front of her.

But she sighed and moved back. She couldn't let Cassandra get to her. There was way too much at stake.

As Mrs Jones barked out more positions, Billie became even more determined. Miss Murphy believed in her; she'd given her a second chance. There was no way she was going to let her down, even if Cassandra was Mrs Jones's pet.

After a few more poses, Mrs Jones rapped her cane on the floor. 'And now a pas de deux,' she announced.

Oh please, please don't put me with Cassandra, Billie silently begged.

'You,' Mrs Jones said, pointing her cane at Billie. 'I want you to dance with Rafael.'

'But . . .' Cassandra blurted.

'I beg your pardon?' Mrs Jones said.

'Nothing, Miss.' Cassandra sulkily made her way to the side of the studio with all the other students.

As Rafael came and stood next to Billie she tried to wipe the fact that he was an international ballet prodigy from her mind. She tried to forget all about the article she'd read about him being the next Mikhail Baryshnikov. He was just a boy, that was all.

'Partnering is about trusting each other, and eye contact is the best way to create that trust,' Mrs Jones said, coming over to them.

Billie stared into Rafael's eyes – and immediately

felt the overwhelming desire to giggle. *Oh my God, what is wrong with you?* she said to herself. *You're about to dance with a ballet prodigy in front of a ballet guru! Now is so not the time for nervous laughter!* She took a deep breath and thankfully managed to keep her composure.

'Rafael, can you support Billie and do two grande jetes to start the pas de deux?' Mrs Jones said.

'Sure,' Rafael replied nonchalantly.

As the music played, Rafael lifted Billie higher than she could ever jump herself. He exuded so much strength and confidence she was able to relax into the movement and not feel scared. She felt like an eagle, soaring through the studio. Then Rafael stood behind her and placed his hands on the small of her back. Billie felt a shiver run up her spine. There was something so sure about him – it made her feel so secure. He lifted her over his head until she was upside down and she performed a split. Billie felt as light as air as he walked her round in a circle. She felt that she could do anything, even fly, when she was dancing with him. As the music finished Rafael looked into her eyes. For the first time ever she felt he'd actually noticed her, but then the moment was gone and he looked away.

'Very good,' Mrs Jones called. 'Next please.'

Just as the rehearsal was coming to a close, someone unlocked the door – and Miss Murphy walked in.

'Mrs Jones, could I just have a quick word with the students please?'

Mrs Jones nodded. 'Of course.'

'I have some very good news, everyone,' Miss Murphy said as they all gathered around. 'A dear friend of mine is choreographing *Swan Lake* at the Royal Opera House this autumn and they've agreed to let you come and see the show – and you're going to have the best seats in the house.'

Everyone's face lit up – including Mrs Jones's. 'How wonderful!' she cried, clapping her hands together in delight.

'I'm hoping that seeing the performance will

inspire you to do your best work for the showcase,' Miss Murphy said.

'Yes!' Mrs Jones exclaimed. 'Make sure you take something from it that you can bring back to your performance. I shall expect great things from you upon your return!'

At lunchtime, Billie headed to the canteen. It was in the Murphy Wing of the Academy, so the walls were all made of glass, allowing loads of natural light to stream in. As well as a huge buffet counter with trays of healthy dishes from all over the world, there was a juice and smoothie bar where you could get fresh drinks made to order. Billie got a salmon salad and a banana and peanut butter smoothie and headed over to Tilly, who was sitting at a table at the back.

'Bill! How did your first rehearsal go?' Tilly asked, before taking a bite of her tuna wrap.

'It was great. Well, it was tough, then great. We have Mrs Jones teaching us.'

Tilly's eyes widened. 'No way! What's she like?'

Billie nodded. 'She's pretty strict. But I like that. She makes you do your best. And something really cool happened at the end of rehearsal. Miss Murphy came to see us and told us that she's going to take us to see *Swan Lake* at the Royal Opera House.'

'Oh my God, that's amazing! How come the ice queen doesn't look happy then?'

Billie followed Tilly's gaze over to Cassandra who was pushing a solitary lettuce leaf round her plate. 'I don't know. She wasn't very happy when Mrs Jones asked me to dance with Rafael.'

'Ha, I bet she wasn't. What was it like?'

'What?'

'Dancing with Rafael?'

Billie felt her face flush and she pretended to look for something in her bag. 'It was good.' She giggled.

'I bet.' Tilly sighed. 'You should see some of the moves he's doing in the street crew. Turns out he's a bit of a capoeira genius as well as a ballet prodigy.'

'Capoeira? The Brazilian martial art?'

'Yep. He has this sick way of combining it with ballet. You should see it.' Tilly looked at her. 'Seriously, we're meeting in the stable after school tonight. Why don't you come along?'

'You just need to use your core in a different way,' Andre said, placing his hands on Billie's hips. 'Forget about the posture, with street dance it's all about letting go and finding your own street beast within. Pretend you're Naomi Campbell strutting down a catwalk . . . that's what I do!'

After Tilly had spent the rest of lunch break persuading her to join them Billie had come to the stable straight from her cleaning and now she was standing in a circle with the rest of the crew. The stable was looking a lot more studio-like now. The storage crates had all been moved out of the way and someone had started a graffiti mural on the main wall.

Billie focused on her hips as Andre gently rocked them back and forth and side to side.

'Feel the beat inside,' Andre said. 'Tilly, can you turn up the volume?'

Billie closed her eyes and felt the beat thudding into her. She started moving her hips in time.

'Good,' Andre said. 'Now give me a roll.'

This time, when Billie tried rolling her spine it felt easier, more natural. She realized she had to stop thinking about it so hard and just let the music take over. She closed her eyes again and it was as if something was unlocking inside of her. The others started to freestyle but Billie danced off to the side. She wasn't confident enough to join them yet, but she didn't feel so intimidated any more either. The showcase audition had taught her a lot. She felt someone grab her hand from behind. It was Rafael. He raised his eyebrows questioningly like he was asking her to dance. Billie felt the same warmth and connection she'd felt dancing with him in the rehearsal so she nodded and followed him back to the centre of the floor. The others whooped and clapped as Rafael started doing the dance they'd shared earlier but throwing in some capoeira moves. Billie's fear lifted – by doing the same dance they'd done earlier he'd given her a way in. She started following his lead. They ended with a triple turn and then Rafael lifted her high. Tilly and Andre cheered with excitement. MJ was staring at them, mesmerized.

'That was beat!' Andre said.

'Yeah, you guys were fierce!' Tilly said.

'Yeah – well done,' MJ muttered, looking at his feet.

'Thank you,' Billie said. She turned to Rafael. 'And thank you.'

Rafael shrugged and gave her a lop-sided grin. 'It is nothing.'

'I do believe we have a crew,' Andre said. 'Il Bello Street Crew is born!'

'Il Bello?' Billie looked at him questioningly.

'Our name,' Andre explained. 'It means "The Beautiful!"'

CHAPTER ELEVEN

'Mum, are you OK?' Billie raced up the office to where her mum, who had been busy cleaning, had slumped down at a desk, her head in her hands.

'I'm sorry, love, I went all dizzy,' her mum said.

'Stay there. I'll get you some water.' As Billie made her way over to the water cooler she felt a wave of panic. Her mum had seemed different lately. Working two jobs meant she was usually tired but now there was something else. She seemed so down. It was as if she'd lost her sparkle. Billie came back over with a plastic cup of water. 'Drink this, I'll do the vacuuming.'

'No! You can't do everything. You must be

exhausted after your day at school. I should never have let you come to help me.'

'I'm fine. Sit there and drink.' But as Billie turned on the vacuum cleaner she felt anything but fine. Over the last couple of weeks the pressure at WEDA had intensified. She was exhausted from classes and homework and cleaning and rehearsals. But her mum had seemed so tired and down lately there was no way she could let her do her cleaning job on her own. Billie pulled out an office chair and started cleaning under a desk. What if her mum was ill? What if she had something seriously wrong with her, like Billie's dad had? She turned the vacuum cleaner off.

'Mum?'

'Yes?'

'Do you think maybe you should see a doctor?'

'What? No!' Her mum immediately looked really stressed. 'I can't see a doctor. I can't get signed off sick. What if I lose my job?' She got up and came over to Billie. 'I'm sorry, love, I didn't mean to snap.

There's nothing wrong with me. I'm just having trouble sleeping lately. It's always tough this time of year.'

Billie nodded as the realization dawned on her. Of course. Why hadn't she remembered? In all the excitement and busyness of getting into WEDA she'd forgotten that her parents' wedding anniversary was approaching.

The next morning, when Billie woke up, she instantly knew something was wrong, she just wasn't sure what. She rubbed her eyes and yawned, trying to get rid of the fog from her brain. Something was definitely wrong, but what? Then, as she realized what it was, she filled with dread. Bright sunlight was streaming in beneath her curtain but it was always dark when her alarm clock went off. Billie sat bolt upright. Her alarm hadn't gone off. She must have been so tired when she went to bed last night she forgot to set it. Billie looked at the time and her stomach lurched. It was gone eight o'clock. Her first class began in less than an hour but it took her two hours to get there. Billie jumped out of bed and rushed to the bathroom. Just as she got there her mum emerged from her bedroom – her eyes red and puffy.

'Billie, why are you still here?'

'I overslept. Are you OK?'

'Yes, yes, I'm fine,' her mum said, turning away. 'Go on, you'd better get ready.'

As Billie cleaned her teeth she felt knotted with tension. She didn't want to leave her mum like this but on the other hand she couldn't miss a day at WEDA – especially not today, when they were having a double rehearsal for the showcase.

'Are you sure you don't want me to stay home with you?' she asked her mum when she came out of the bathroom.

'Of course not!' her mum replied. 'I'm fine. I just – I had a bad dream, that's all.'

By the time Billie got to the academy her ballet class was midway through. She knew there was no point even trying to join them – the studio doors were always locked once a class began to avoid the students being interrupted mid-barre-work. Billie sat down on the floor outside and tried to compose herself.

'Billie! What are you doing?'

Billie scrambled to her feet. Miss Murphy was coming down the corridor towards her.

'I – uh – I was late getting in. I . . . I overslept.'

'You overslept?' Miss Murphy did not look impressed.

Billie noticed a movement out of the corner of her eye and saw Cassandra watching them through the viewing window of the studio.

'Yes, I –'

'Oversleeping is not really the behaviour of someone who is dedicated to their dance, Billie.'

'I am dedicated, I just . . .' Billie wanted to kick herself. Why had she said she'd overslept? She should have just blamed her lateness on the trains.

'I really do expect better from you.'

'I'm sorry.' Billie hung her head in shame. 'It won't happen again.'

'Good.' Miss Murphy turned and carried on walking up the corridor, her heels clicking on the polished floor.

Billie looked back at the viewing window. Cassandra gave her a smug smirk before turning back to the class.

By the time lunch break came around Billie couldn't get to the stable fast enough. It was weird thinking that she'd been so reluctant to join the crew at first – now it was the only place she felt she could truly relax.

'Billie! Oh my days, what are you wearing?' Andre exclaimed as he let her in.

'I overslept. I had to get dressed in a rush,' Billie said, as she looked down at her drab grey sweatshirt and faded leggings.

'Hmm, looks like you had to get dressed in the middle of a jumble sale! What have you done with your Inner Fashionista?' Andre shook his head. 'Never mind, at least you're here. We need your mighty word power.'

'What do you mean?' Billie followed Andre over to the others, who were all sitting in a circle beneath the graffiti mural, which now took up most of the wall and featured cartoon-style pictures of them all dancing.

'Oh wow, who did that?' Billie exclaimed.

'I did,' Tilly said shyly. 'Do you like it?'

'I love it!' Billie said.

'The girl has skills,' Andre said.

'It's very good,' MJ muttered.

'It's cool,' Raf said.

Tilly grinned from ear to ear. 'Thanks, guys.'

Billie sat down in between Raf and Tilly.

'Hey,' Raf said, smiling at her. 'Are you looking forward to *Swan Lake* tonight?'

'Oh yes,' Billie said, feeling a shiver of excitement just thinking about it. 'I can't believe I'll be going to the Opera House to actually see the whole thing.'

Raf frowned. 'What do you mean?'

'I've only ever been able to afford to go in the slips before, but the view's really rubbish there, you can only see half the stage.'

'Yeah and usually the half where nothing's happening,' Tilly said. 'You guys are so lucky.'

'I bet it'll be awesome,' MJ said, still looking at the mural. He didn't really do eye contact but in the last couple of weeks he'd become way more talkative. Of course, Andre was taking all the credit.

'So why do you need my mighty word power?' Billie asked.

'We're trying to come up with a slogan for Il Bello,' Andre explained.

'A slogan?'

Andre nodded. 'Yeah. You know, like Nike have "*Just do it*" And McDonalds have "*I'm lovin' it*". We need something that sums up our ethos. Think, guys. What are we about?'

Tilly's brow furrowed in thought. 'Keeping it real?'

Andre nodded. 'Yep, for sure.'

'Being brave?' Billie suggested, thinking of how much fear she'd had to overcome to join the crew.

'Absolutely,' Andre said. 'So we've got keeping it real and being brave. Anything else?'

'Being authentic,' Raf suggested.

Billie couldn't help smiling. MJ wasn't the only one who had changed. In the past couple of weeks Raf had become a whole lot friendlier too – in the street crew at least. It was the only place she saw him look truly interested and engaged.

'Yes!' Andre exclaimed. 'Il Bello is all about being authentic. How about: be you, be brave, be authentic?'

'I like it,' Tilly said.

'Is there a better word for brave though?' Andre said. 'I feel like that sounds like the kind of thing a mum would tell her little kid, like, "be a brave soldier".'

Billie laughed. 'Good point.'

'What about fearless?' Tilly said.

'Yes!' the others exclaimed in unison.

'Great word,' Andre said.

'Seriously?' Tilly looked around at them, clearly chuffed.

'See, you are good at words after all,' Billie said, causing Tilly to grin even wider.

'Be you, be fearless, be authentic,' Andre said.

'I like it,' MJ said matter-of-factly.

'Yeah, it's cool,' Raf said.

'The three Bs,' Billie said.

Tilly jumped to her feet and fetched a can of spray paint from her bag. The others watched as she started painting some words at the top of the mural.

THE THREE BEEZ.

'Love it!' Andre said.

Then Tilly painted the outline of a bumble bee wearing a gold baseball cap with a chain. *BEE REAL*, she sprayed in a speech bubble coming from its mouth.

'Tilly, that's brilliant!' Billie said.

Tilly did a pretend bow, then carried on with her work.

Billie hugged her knees to her chest and felt a warm glow inside. The day might have got off to a terrible start but now, thanks to the crew, she felt great again. And, tonight she would be seeing *Swan Lake* at the Royal Opera House. Maybe life wasn't so bad after all.

The last class of the day seemed to go on forever, but finally it came to an end. Billie decided to call her mum and check she was OK before going down to the changing rooms to get ready for *Swan Lake*. The academy had arranged for a minibus to take them to the Opera House and they were meeting outside reception when they were ready. But as soon as her mum answered the phone Billie's heart sank. Her usually cheery voice was heavy and dull.

'Mum, are you OK?' Billie asked. She spotted Cassandra hovering, clearly eavesdropping and turned away.

There was a moment's silence before her

mum replied. 'I got a warning from my boss at the cafe today.'

'What? Why?'

'I left some eggs frying for too long and the pan caught fire.'

'Oh, Mum, are you OK? Is the cafe OK?'

'Yes. Thankfully Tony was there and managed to put it out before the whole kitchen went up.'

'That must have been so scary.'

'I don't know what's wrong with me,' her mum said, her voice trembling.

'Right, I'm coming straight home,' Billie said.

'But isn't tonight your trip to *Swan Lake?*'

'Yes, but that's OK. I can see *Swan Lake* any time.'

'No, Billie.' Her mum's voice was firmer now. 'You've been looking forward to this for so long. I won't have you miss it for me. I'll be fine, I promise.'

Billie sighed. 'Are you sure?'

'Yes, absolutely. I'm just really tired. I think I'm going to phone in sick to the cleaning job and get an early night.'

Billie frowned, unsure of what to do.

'Seriously, love, you go and enjoy the show and I'll go straight to bed. Is that a deal?'

'OK, deal.'

'But you have to promise me you'll give me a full review of the show in the morning.'

'OK, will do!'

Billie hung up, feeling worried, and went over to the window. The sun was beginning to set behind the trees, streaking the sky tangerine and crimson. She sighed, still unsure of what to do. She was relieved her mum wouldn't be going to work tonight, but pretty shaken up about the fire. What if her mum had got seriously hurt? The text notification went off on her phone.

I really do want you to go to the ballet tonight. It's way too good an opportunity to miss. And don't forget I expect a full report in the morning. Love, Mum xxxx

Billie breathed a sigh of relief. Outside, she saw the minibus winding its way up the drive. She picked up her bag and started hurrying towards the stairs to get ready.

By the time Billie got down to the girls' changing rooms, the others had all been and gone, leaving a cloud of perfume in their wake. Billie quickly pulled her dress from her bag and put it on. She brushed her hair, applied a quick coat of lip-gloss and looked at her reflection in the mirror. 'You're going to see *Swan Lake!*' she whispered. 'You're going to see all of it!'

She picked up her bag and headed for the door. But when she turned the handle the door wouldn't budge. She tried it again, harder this time. Then she pulled so hard she thought the handle might come off in her hand. But the door still wouldn't open. Billie stepped backwards, staring at it in shock. It was locked! She fished her phone from her bag and tried calling Tilly. But the changing rooms were down in the basement of the academy and there was no reception . . .

Billie looked around the deserted changing rooms, panic-stricken. She was stuck down here with no way of getting help – and no way of making it to the minibus!

CHAPTER TWELVE

'Help!' Billie banged on the door and yelled until her hand stung and her throat was raw. But no one came. No one would be coming down here until classes started again tomorrow. She was trapped, and would miss the show. Billie's heart sank. And then she had a panicked thought. What would her mum say when she woke up in the morning to discover Billie hadn't come home? She was so stressed as it was, any benefits from taking the night off work would be gone.

Billie started pacing up and down. The caretaker, Ted, must have locked the door when he was doing his after-school rounds. But why didn't he check there was no one in there? Billie thought of the others in her rehearsal group. They'd be on their way to London by now. Her stomach lurched as she thought of Miss Murphy. What would she think of her non-appearance? And the same day she was late to classes because she overslept.

'Why is this happening to me?' Billie wailed. Then, just when she thought all hope was lost, she heard the sound of footsteps in the corridor outside.

'Help! Help!' she yelled, pummelling the door.

'Oh my God, Billie, is that you?' Tilly shouted from the other side of the door.

Relief washed through Billie at the sound of her friend's voice.

'Tilly! Yes, I've been locked in!'

'Oh jeez! I knew something was up. OK, don't worry. I'll go and get Ted.'

'Thank you!'

As Tilly's footsteps faded back up the corridor, Billie leaned against the wall and sighed with relief. She might have lost her chance of going to the show, but at least she'd be able to get home and save her mum from a major stress-out.

After what seemed like forever, but was probably only a couple of minutes, Billie heard the sound of a key in the lock.

'Billie, love, I'm so sorry!' Ted said, coming into the changing rooms, followed closely by Tilly. 'She said no one was down here, that you'd all gone home.'

'Who said?' Billie asked, picking up her bag.

'One of the girls.'

Billie's skin prickled with suspicion. 'Which girl?'

'I don't know her name. Long dark hair, very pale blue eyes.'

'Cassandra!' Billie and Tilly both exclaimed.

'Come on,' Tilly said, grabbing Billie's arm. 'You've got a show to go to.'

'But I missed the minibus!'

'You've still got time if you get the train.'

'Oh, I don't know . . .'

Tilly frowned at her. 'I thought you were supposed to be a hardcore ballerina.'

'I am but –'

'No buts, it's *Swan Lake*.'

'But I don't have my ticket. Miss Murphy has them.'

'Yes, and Andre can text her and tell her what happened.'

'But –'

'Go!' Tilly exclaimed. 'I'll get Andre to get Miss M to call you so you can sort out the ticket.'

'Thank you!' Billie was about to leave then stopped and turned. 'How did you know I was down here?'

'I overheard Cassandra telling Miss M that you couldn't make it to the show and something felt wrong.'

'She did *what*?'

Tilly nudged Billie in the direction of the stairs. 'Just go – we can sort all that out in the morning.'

'OK. Thank you.' Billie picked up her bag and started to run.

*

All the way into London, Billie burned with indignation about Cassandra. Her telling Ted that the changing room was empty could have been an innocent mistake, but why had she told Miss Murphy that she couldn't come to see *Swan Lake*? When she got out of the Underground she had a text from Andre telling her Miss Murphy had left her ticket at the box office.

Can't believe you got locked in!
Some people get all the drama! Xoxo

Billie got to her seat just as the lights were dimming.

'Where were you?' Raf whispered from the seat next to hers.

'Long story!' she whispered back but then all thoughts of being locked in the changing room and Cassandra's games were wiped from her mind as she was sucked into the world of the ballet. As she looked around at the thick, crimson curtains and ornate golden ceiling she felt years of dancing history seeping into her. Seeing it from the front of the auditorium made such a difference. Without the distraction of a pillar obscuring the view, Billie was able to absorb herself fully. Watching the ballerinas took her breath away. Their grace and precision in pointe shoes was incredible. They never made mistakes or even gave the slightest wobble. It was awe-inspiring. She thought of all the ballerinas who'd danced on that stage before – a chain of dancers reaching back in time. Would she one day be part of that chain? She really hoped so. Billie felt a fizz of excitement run up her spine. She couldn't wait to get back to WEDA. From now on she was going to double her efforts to do well in the showcase. No, scrap that, she was going to quadruple-double them! Whatever it took to one day dance on that stage.

When Billie woke up the next morning – to two alarms, one on her phone, one on her clock – she was still buzzing from the show. She got out of bed and crept along the hallway. She didn't want to wake her mum if she was still sleeping.

'Billie,' her mum called as one of the floorboards creaked.

'I'm sorry, Mum, I was trying not to wake you,' Billie said, coming into her bedroom. The floor was covered with boxes of her dad's belongings and there was a pile of his old journals on her mum's bedside table.

'Don't be silly. I've been waiting for you to get up. How was it? Come here.' Her mum pulled back the duvet and Billie slipped into the bed next to her. 'Oh, Mum, it was so beautiful. Seriously, I could hardly breathe.'

'Just think, it could be you dancing there one day,' her mum said with a smile.

'Oh I don't know – they're so good!'

'So are you! You wouldn't be at WEDA if you weren't.' She put her arm round Billie. 'I'm so proud of you.'

'How are you feeling today? Did you sleep well?' Billie looked at her anxiously.

'I'm OK. I've decided to take today off too. I'm just so tired.'

'Good. Hopefully some rest will make you feel better,' Billie said.

Her mum nodded. 'Right, well you'd better get ready. Don't want to be late two days running.'

'No, definitely not!' Billie got up and walked over to the door. 'Love you, Mum.'

'Love you too, sweetheart.'

On the way into WEDA, Billie had vowed to confront Cassandra as soon as possible about what she'd said to Miss Murphy. It turned out she didn't have to wait long, as Cassandra was walking through the reception area just as Billie arrived.

'Hey,' Billie called.

'What?' Cassandra said frostily.

'Why did you tell Miss Murphy that I couldn't come on the trip last night?' To Billie's surprise Cassandra didn't look in the least bit guilty. Instead she stared at her defiantly.

'Because I heard you telling your mum you weren't going to go on the phone. And then when you didn't turn up to the minibus I thought it was only right that I should tell Miss Murphy what I'd heard. I was just trying to help,' she added, with one of her extra smug smiles.

'I didn't turn up to the minibus because I'd been locked in the changing room,' Billie replied, studying Cassandra's face for any flicker of guilt. But again there was nothing – only shock.

'What? But how?'

'You told the caretaker it was empty, that it was OK to go ahead and lock up.'

'But it was empty when I left it, and I'd assumed you'd gone home to be with your mum.'

'So you didn't see me going down there?'

Cassandra frowned. 'Of course not. Honestly, Billie, you're starting to sound really paranoid. Are you sure you're cut out for life at WEDA?'

'What's that supposed to mean?' But before Cassandra could answer, the bell rang for registration.

'Better get a move on,' Cassandra said patronisingly. 'You don't want to be late yet again!' And with a swish of her hair she strode off down the corridor.

At lunchtime, Billie hung around her locker for a few minutes before making her way to the stable. The crew had organized it so that none of them would walk down there at the same time as it might raise suspicions. Billie was extra careful not to be seen as she made her way towards the shelter of the trees. The last thing she needed was to get into trouble again. Andre and Tilly were already in the stable when she got there, looking up at the mural. Tilly had added another two 'beez' flying above the pictures of the crew – one saying bee *fearless* and one saying bee *authentic* and all equally full of swag.

'It looks amazing,' Billie said, as she came to stand next to them.

'Thank you.' Tilly grinned.

Billie loved the way Tilly was when she was here

with the crew – she was so much more relaxed than she was in their lessons.

'Hey,' MJ muttered as he entered the stable. He was wearing his usual signature look of vest top, pinstripe trousers and fedora.

'Hey, MJ!' Andre said. 'You're looking mighty fine today.'

'I think we need to feature him on Spotted,' Tilly said.

'Absolutely.' Andre nodded.

Billie couldn't help sighing as she wondered if they'd ever want to feature her. Despite Andre's style advice, she still didn't feel as cool as the other members of the crew. Just like with her dance, she knew she had a way to go before she truly found her swag.

The door opened and Raf walked in. As always, he looked effortlessly cool. From the way he walked to his low-slung jeans and the prayer beads around his neck.

'Right, now we're all here, I wanted to run an

idea by you,' Andre said as they gathered round. 'I was thinking it would be cool if we choreographed a new routine together – something to express our three Bs ethos.'

'Great idea,' Tilly said.

'Thank you, I'm full of them,' Andre quipped.

'Hmm, full of something,' Raf muttered but he was grinning.

Andre went over to the sound system and started playing a track. 'Why don't we all just freestyle and see what comes? Think about what being fearless and authentic means to you and express it in your dance.'

Billie focused on the beats of the music and started bobbing her head in time. The rest of her body started to let go and follow suit, spurring a rocking motion that started in her shoulders and ended in her hips. She loosened her pelvis and started rocking back and forth. Now she'd finally overcome her block it was so much easier to get into the rhythm. Once she'd fully loosened up she thought about what it means to be fearless. She pictured herself completely unafraid, and instinctively she closed her eyes. Fusing her love of contemporary with a street twist she let go of her insecurities and popped her shoulders and arms to the beat, moving from one foot to another.

Next to her, Tilly started voguing, using her hands to accentuate the beats. MJ started doing a pencil turn – spinning with both feet together and Andre dropped down low to the ground, shuffling his feet and whacking his arms in and out. For a long time Raf had his eyes closed, just grooving to the beat, then suddenly he fell to the ground, catching himself on one arm with his legs out doing a six step, then freezing with his feet off the ground.

'All right!' Andre yelled in encouragement. 'You guys are slaying it!'

Billie felt as if her whole body was smiling with relief as her insecurities washed away and her body let go even more. She'd always thought that nothing would feel as good as ballet, but street dancing was opening up a whole new level of joy. It was so freeing to be able to let go like this, so much more expressive having so many new emotions to explore.

All too soon, the alarm went off on Andre's phone, signalling the end to lunch. 'Thanks so much, guys. You gave everything and more,' Andre said as he switched off the music. 'Next meet-up we start putting together a routine. Now we'd better get to lessons.'

Instantly, Tilly's face fell. 'Oh no, we've got English.'

Billie put her arm round her. 'Don't worry, you know I'll help you.'

'It's not that I'm worried about, it's getting our homework assignments back,' Tilly said with a frown.

When Billie and Tilly got to English the lesson was about to begin.

'Tut, tut, almost late again,' Cassandra said, as Billie walked past. 'Where do you two disappear off to every lunchtime, anyway?'

Billie's heart began to pound. There was no way Cassandra could find out about the street crew. If she found out she'd tell the teachers for sure. And Billie couldn't afford to let Miss Murphy down again.

'None of your business,' Tilly retorted. 'We don't hang around with snobs.'

'Don't talk to me like that,' Cassandra hissed.

'Why not? Who do you think you are?' Tilly snapped.

Billie pulled on her sleeve. 'Come on, it's not worth it,' she whispered.

Tilly sighed then went and sat down at their table, glaring at Cassandra the whole time.

'OK, class, settle down please,' Mrs Jarvis said, picking up a pile of papers. 'I've marked your homework assignments. Could someone please hand them out for me?'

Cassandra's arm shot up. 'I'll do it, Miss.'

Billie frowned. It was unlike Cassandra to volunteer to do something so menial.

'Today, we're going to be reading the first chapter of George Orwell's *1984*,' Mrs Jarvis said. 'This is the text we'll be studying for the rest of this term.'

'Oh joy, a whole book,' Tilly muttered. 'I thought poems were bad enough, but at least they only go on for about a page.'

'Billie,' Cassandra said in a sickly sweet voice as she placed Billie's paper down in front of her.

Billie felt excitement and relief as she saw the letter A circled in red at the top of the page. She'd got an A for her first English assignment!

'And Tilly,' Cassandra said, placing a paper in front of Tilly. 'I take it the D stands for dunce,' she whispered, bending closer to Tilly.

'Shut up!' Tilly yelled and she lightly shoved Cassandra on the shoulder.

'Ow!' Cassandra screamed, staggering backwards theatrically and crashing into the table behind her.

'What on earth's going on?' Mrs Jarvis said, jumping to her feet.

'She pushed me,' Cassandra wailed, rubbing her shoulder.

'It wasn't that hard,' Tilly said. 'She's faking it, Miss.'

'Did you push Cassandra, Tilly?' Mrs Jarvis said, marching towards them.

'Yes, but –'

'Mrs Jones's office, now.'

'But –'

Mrs Jarvis's face was red with anger. 'Now, Tilly. I told you before, I won't tolerate that kind of behaviour in my classroom. If you won't listen to me, maybe you'll listen to Mrs Jones.'

Billie watched, horrified, as Tilly got her things together and stood up to leave.

'Are you all right, Cassandra?' Mrs Jarvis asked.

'Yes, I think so,' Cassandra said, biting on her bottom lip as if she was trying to stop herself crying.

Billie tutted.

'Is everything all right, Billie, or do you need to go and see Mrs Jones too?' Mrs Jarvis said.

Billie shook her head and looked down at

151

the desk, trying to look calm, but inside she was seething. Now she was certain that Cassandra had tried to make her miss the trip to *Swan Lake*, just as she had tried to unsettle her before the audition for the showcase. And now Tilly might end up getting expelled because of her. As Mrs Jarvis began talking about George Orwell Billie couldn't concentrate at all. All of her words were drowned out by the angry hum of Billie's thoughts. Cassandra shouldn't be allowed to behave like this, it was totally unfair.

At the end of the lesson, Mrs Jarvis asked Cassandra to stay behind to help her collect up the books. As the rest of the class hurried off to their next class, Billie hung back, waiting for her in the corridor.

'What do you want?' Cassandra said, when she finally appeared.

'You had no right talking to Tilly like that,' Billie said.

'Actually, I have every right,' Cassandra hissed back.

'Really? How did you work that out?'

'If it weren't for scholarship paupers like you and Tilly sucking up funds, things would be so much better around here. Do you have any idea how much money my father has to donate to WEDA to keep this place maintained?'

Billie's face burned.

Cassandra leaned in closer. 'Miss Murphy might have some obsession with helping charity cases like you but none of the other staff want you here. Mrs Jones can't stand having to pay out so much to subsidize you.'

All of the anger that had been bubbling away inside of Billie came rushing out. 'You think you're so great, don't you, just because your parents have money,' she snapped. 'But do you know what? I'd rather be poor for the rest of my life than be a horrible spoiled brat like you.'

To Billie's surprise, Cassandra's eyes widened in shock. She looked genuinely hurt. Then they filled with tears. Billie felt a stab of panic. Had she gone too far? Had she been too mean?

'Billie!'

Billie froze at the sound of Miss Murphy's voice right behind her.

'I don't know why she's being like this, Miss Murphy,' Cassandra sobbed. 'I can't help it if my parents are rich.'

'That's OK, Cassandra,' Miss Murphy said. 'You get to your next class. Billie, stay here.'

Billie watched as Cassandra walked off down the corridor, head bowed, still sobbing loudly. She felt sick as she realized what had just happened. Cassandra must have seen Miss Murphy coming and turned on the tears.

'I can explain,' she began but Miss Murphy held up her hand, gesturing at her to be quiet.

'I am very, very disappointed in you, Billie. First you turn up late to your lessons because you oversleep, then you almost miss last night's show and now this.'

'But –'

Miss Murphy shook her head. 'There is a zero tolerance policy at WEDA when it comes to bullying behaviour. Do you understand? *Zero* tolerance. I don't ever want to catch you talking to anyone like that again.'

Billie nodded, tears of anger and frustration burning at the corners of her eyes. As she watched Miss Murphy walk away she felt overwhelmed with despair. Not only had Cassandra got away with her fake tears but Billie had disappointed Miss Murphy yet again. She looked at the framed pictures of the ballerinas lining the walls of the corridor. They all looked so poised and had achieved so much but the price it cost to get to that level was intense. For the first time ever, Billie started wondering if she should give up dance entirely. It was a horrible feeling. Her dream of becoming a professional ballerina had been her life raft for years – something to cling to when times got tough. What would she do without it? She felt so lost and alone. It was at times like these she wished her dad would appear and swoop her up into his arms. He'd know what to do in a situation like this. He'd make her feel better. But he wasn't there – and he never would be again. And even worse, Billie was having to fill in for him, supporting her mum and being the strong one at home. She picked up her bag and trudged down the corridor, aching with sadness.

CHAPTER THIRTEEN

That night when Billie got home she found her mum sitting on the living-room sofa surrounded by albums of her wedding photos.

'Hello, love, how was your day?' her mum asked flatly.

'It was great,' Billie lied. There was no way she could tell her what had happened and add to her stress.

'Do you want any tea?' her mum asked. 'There's a ready-meal in the fridge.'

This was another sign that things were badly wrong – her mum was no longer cooking at home. Normally she loved to cook. It was as if she was losing her interest in everything – apart from Billie's dad.

Billie looked down at the photos. 'He's not coming back, Mum.' Her eyes filled with tears. 'No matter how many times you look at the photos.'

'I know but –'

'I'm really tired. I think I'll go to bed.' Billie waited for a moment, hoping her mum would tell her to come and sit with her, ask her to watch a movie like they used to, but her mum just smiled at her sadly.

'OK, love, good night.'

When Billie got to her room she flung herself on her bed and started pounding her pillow. 'Why did you have to get sick? Why did you have to leave us?' she cried angrily but quietly, so her mum wouldn't hear. Then she immediately felt guilty for getting angry at her dad. 'We need you,' she sobbed. '*I* need you. I need someone to talk to.'

Finally, when there were no more tears left, she sat up and reached for the notepad and pen on her bedside table. Her Uncle Charlie always said that writing poems was better than therapy, that it helped him make sense of the world and get things off his chest. Billie decided to give it a try – it wasn't as if she had anything to lose. She wrote the words TO DAD across the top of a clean page and let the words pour from her.

TO DAD
Do you hear me when I cry?
Can you hear me asking why?
Do you see me when I dance?
Would you hold me if you had the chance?
What would you tell us if you could?
Why did you have to leave for good?
Will I ever stop wishing for then?
Will I ever see you again?

Billie lay back and sighed. Tears spilled from her eyes and rolled down her face but this time they weren't angry tears. Uncle Charlie was right, there was something about writing the questions that made her feel better. Now they were set down on the page in a poem they were no longer tangled up in an angry knot inside her head. Billie turned off her light and closed her eyes. 'I love you, Dad,' she whispered into the darkness.

The next morning Billie got to the academy an hour before classes started. Andre had texted the night before to ask the crew to meet for an early morning practice. But as Billie made her way through the trees she didn't feel the normal tingle of excitement as the stable came into view. Instead she felt heavy-hearted. She'd done some serious thinking on the way into WEDA about how she could try to turn things around and she'd come to a really depressing conclusion.

'Hey!' Andre said as Billie let herself in.

The others were already dancing. Billie breathed a sigh of relief when she saw Tilly.

'Billie!' Tilly said, dancing over to her.

'How did it go with Mrs Jones?' Billie asked.

'On a scale of one to ten – minus one gazillion.

But the good news is, I'm still here; the bad news is, I'm on report.'

'What does that mean?' Billie asked.

'It means my every move is being watched. So I won't be able to dunk Cassandra into a vat of cold porridge.'

'Or shave her hair off and dye her scalp green,' Andre added.

'We were coming up with ways to get revenge last night in Andre's dorm room,' Tilly explained.

'Enough about her, let's dance,' Andre said, taking Billie's hand.

'I–I'm not going to be able to,' Billie stammered, looking down at the floor.

'Why not?' Andre said.

'Yes, why?' Raf asked, stopping dancing and staring at her.

'I'm going to have to leave Il Bello.' Billie felt sick as she heard herself speak the words out loud.

'No way!' Tilly exclaimed.

'Over my dead body!' Andre exclaimed, then he

frowned. 'OK, maybe not literally but Billie? Seriously? You're only just finding your inner street beast.'

'I got into trouble again yesterday,' Billie said.

'Who with?' Andre asked.

'Your mum.'

He raised his eyebrows. 'What for?'

'Yelling at Cassandra and making her cry.'

'Wait, what? You made the ice queen cry?' Tilly stared at her.

'Fake tears. I was telling her what I thought of her after she got you into trouble and she saw Miss Murphy coming and started to cry.' Billie sighed. 'So now Miss Murphy thinks I'm a bully as well as everything else.'

'But that's so unfair!' Tilly cried.

'I'll speak to her,' Andre said.

Billie shook her head. 'No. It's not just what happened yesterday. She caught me coming in late because I overslept and then I almost missed *Swan Lake*. I just don't want to risk getting into trouble again.'

'But you're one of us now!' Tilly said.

'I know. I'm sorry. But I can't take the risk. There's stuff going on at home too.' Billie's eyes filled with tears.

'It's OK,' Tilly said, putting her arm round her. 'You have to do what you have to do.'

'Yeah, I guess,' Andre said, but he couldn't hide his disappointment.

To make things even worse, Billie's first class of the day was acrobatics.

'Let's see if you can crack that aerial cartwheel today, Billie,' Mr Marlo said as they all took their places in front of their mats.

Come on, you can do this, Billie tried telling herself, but her inner voice sounded completely unconvincing. She took a run-up, threw herself over – and yet again, her hand instinctively reached for the mat.

'You've got this, Billie, you just need to believe,' Mr Marlo said.

Billie prepared for another attempt. 'Come on!' she muttered under her breath. 'Be fearless.' But thinking of Il Bello only filled her with disappointment. The truth was, she wasn't fearless. She'd left the crew because she was too afraid of getting into trouble. Even though dancing with them was where she felt most alive and most authentic. She didn't have what it took to do an aerial cartwheel. She probably didn't have what it took to be at WEDA. Billie launched herself forwards and once again, as she went over, she reached her hand out and touched the mat.

'Never mind,' Mr Marlo said. 'Maybe it'll be third time lucky.'

Billie's head began to pound. 'I can't do it. I can't stop my hand from touching the mat.'

Mr Marlo sighed. 'Oh dear, what did we say last time about that word?'

Billie became aware of everyone in the gym hall turning to look. The pounding in her head got louder and louder. 'Please. I can't . . .' she whispered.

'Billie,' Mr Marlo said, warningly.

'I can't! I cant!' Billie snapped, all of her pent-up frustration spilling out.

'Forty press-ups, please,' Mr Marlo said. 'Now.'

Billie got down on her mat, her entire body burning with shame and embarrassment. As she got to twenty press-ups her arms started to ache but she kept on pushing through. She wanted to hurt. She was so angry and frustrated at herself. When she finally completed the set, she sat back on her heels, sweating. Mr Marlo came over and crouched down beside her. 'All of those emotions you've got going on in there,' he said, tapping her lightly on the head, 'learn to channel them into your dance instead of letting them come out your mouth.'

Billie nodded.

'Let me show you something.' Mr Marlo went over to a nearby mat and performed a flawless aerial cartwheel. 'See? Your hand doesn't need to touch the mat. The only thing making you do it is your lack of belief. You need to believe, Billie, understand?'

Billie nodded.

'OK, good. Now go get some lunch.'

As Billie sat down on her own in the canteen she thought of Il Bello practising in the stable and felt a wistful pang.

'Well, look who it is,' Cassandra said as she plonked her tray down opposite her. The only thing on it was an apple and a bottle of water.

Billie ignored her and took a forkful of pasta.

'Comfort eating?' Cassandra said, nodding towards Billie's plate.

'What? No! Why would I be comfort eating?'

'Oh, I don't know,' Cassandra said breezily. 'Having no one to sit with at lunch . . . getting into trouble with Miss Murphy . . . being the *only* person at WEDA who can't do an aerial cartwheel.'

As Cassandra continued to smirk, anger began building inside of Billie. And then something her dad once said to her popped into her mind. It was when she was five years old and just starting school.

'You must always stand up to bullies, Billie. Don't ever let anyone put you down.' Billie felt a shiver run up her spine. She recalled his words so clearly it was as if her dad was right behind her, speaking them into her ear. She looked at Cassandra, still smirking in front of her and then she picked up her plate and tipped her pasta all over Cassandra's head.

'What the –?' Cassandra yelled as a pasta shell slid down her hair, leaving a tomatoey trail.

Shocked gasps followed by ripples of laughter spread through the canteen – and then there was a deathly silence.

'My office, now, Billie.'

Billie turned and saw Miss Murphy marching over to the door.

'I'm pulling you from the showcase,' Miss Murphy said as soon as Billie walked into her office.

'What? But –'

'You're not ready for the pressures of a big show.' Miss Murphy paused and looked Billie right in the eye. 'And maybe you never will be.'

'But I –'

'Becoming a professional dancer is as much about attitude as it is about ability,' Miss Murphy interrupted. 'You need to be able to handle stress. You need to channel your emotions into the dance – not into throwing food over people. I want you to think long and hard about your behaviour these past few days and I want to see a marked improvement.'

Billie nodded, but inside she felt like yelling. It all felt so unfair.

'That will be all.' Miss Murphy went over to the door and held it open for her.

Billie trudged over. 'I'm sorry I let you down,' she mumbled before hurrying off along the corridor.

CHAPTER
FOURTEEN

Even though it was a Saturday, Billie had set her alarm to go off extra early. As she turned on her bedside lamp she saw Uncle Charlie's poem propped against it. She'd put it there the night before as a reminder to be positive and strong. Today she wasn't going to think about WEDA. She wasn't going to let herself get angry about Cassandra. And she wasn't going to feel upset about no longer being in the show. Today was her parents' wedding anniversary and she was going to focus solely on her mum.

Billie got out of bed and pulled on a hoodie and pair of jeans. Then she stuffed her purse into her pocket. She crept along the hallway of the flat, extra careful not to make a sound outside her mum's room, and let herself out of the front door. Outside, the estate was still steeped in darkness. Billie made her way to the glowing light of Mr Patel's convenience store. He always opened early to take in the newspaper delivery. As she walked along the litter-strewn footpath she silently pleaded that he'd have what she was looking for.

'Yes!' Billie exclaimed as she scanned the bucket of flowers outside the shop. Among the carnations and bunches of wilting lilies there was a single bouquet of white roses. It was as if Billie's dad had magically placed them there – he'd always bought her mum white roses on their anniversary. Billie took the bouquet and went inside.

'Morning, Billie,' Mr Patel called from behind the counter. 'You're up bright and early for a weekend.'

Billie laughed. 'Yes, I'm planning a surprise for my mum, so I had to get up before she did.'

'Ah, that's lovely. She's a wonderful woman, your mum.' Mr Patel smiled fondly. 'Is there anything else you need?'

'Just a card.' Billie scanned the revolving card stand. It had to be something positive but without being overly happy. Something hopeful. Her gaze fell on a picture of a beautiful bird, perched on the branch of a tree. Instantly, Billie remembered the Emily Dickinson poem about hope. It was perfect.

Back in the flat Billie heard the click of her mum's light switch. She quickly wrote a message in the card and put the flowers in a vase. She had to give them to her mum before she got up, that's what her dad always used to do. She hurried down the hallway and knocked on the bedroom door.

'Yes,' her mum called.

Billie opened the door. 'I – uh – I got you these.' She placed the roses on her mum's bedside table and looked at her anxiously. It had seemed like such a good idea when she'd first had it, but what if the roses upset her mum? What if it was too painful a reminder?

Her mum gasped and sat upright in the bed.

'Oh, Billie, they're beautiful. They're just like the roses your dad always got me.'

'I know. That's why I chose them.'

Her mum's eyes filled with tears but to Billie's relief she was smiling. 'Thank you. Thank you so much.'

'I got you a card too.' Billie handed her the envelope. 'It reminded me of a poem we did in English recently, all about hope. I wrote the first stanza inside.'

Billie sat down on the bed as her mum opened the card. '*Hope is the thing with feathers,*' she read out loud. '*That perches in the soul. And sings the tune without the words. And never stops at all.* Oh, Billie, that's so beautiful.'

Billie gave a relieved smile.

'I'm sorry I've been so down lately,' her mum said. 'When you said what you did to me the other night – about the photos – I knew I needed to get some help. So I went to see the doctor yesterday and he diagnosed me with mild depression.'

Billie took hold of her hand and clasped it tightly. 'Oh, Mum. I'm so sorry.'

'No, it's fine. To be honest, in a weird way it was a relief. He prescribed me some medication which should have me feeling a lot better really soon and he's referred me to have some grief counselling over your dad. I should have had it years ago. It's so much better to express yourself when you're feeling sad than keep it bottled up.' Her mum got out of bed and took Billie's hand. 'Come with me.'

Billie followed her mum into the kitchen and over to their dream-board. She watched as her mum carefully took down the picture of her dad.

'But that's your favourite picture of him!' Billie exclaimed.

'Don't worry. I'm not getting rid of it, I'm just going to put it somewhere else. That board's meant to represent our future, Billie, not our past.' She smiled bravely through her tears.

Billie wrapped her arms around her and hugged her tight. 'I love you, Mum.'

'Oh, Billie, I love you too.'

'OK, what next, *Step Up* or *Dirty Dancing?*' her mum asked, flicking through the movies on the TV.

'Hmm, I'm thinking *Dirty Dancing,*' Billie replied. 'We haven't done our duet to "The Time of My Life" for ages.'

'Great choice,' her mum said, scrolling down. 'Could you put the lamp on? It's starting to get dark.'

Billie got up, pulled the curtains and turned on the lamp. It was gone five o'clock and she and her mum had spent the entire day under the duvet on the sofa eating popcorn and watching their favourite dance movies. After all the recent stress at WEDA it had been wonderful being cocooned in her fleecy tiger onesie and the fictional worlds of dance where things always worked out in the end. Just as the opening scene from *Dirty Dancing* began playing there was a knock on the door.

'Are you expecting anyone?' Billie asked.

Her mum shook her head.

There was another knock, louder this time.

'I'll go,' Billie said, getting to her feet.

As Billie opened the door she gasped. All of Il Bello were crowded around the doorstep! Well, all of Il Bello apart from MJ, who was hovering behind the others on the pavement.

'Wh-what are you doing here?' she stammered.

'We were worried about you,' Tilly said.

'Is your phone switched off?' Andre asked.

'Yes, I –'

'What is the point in mobile communication if you refuse to communicate?' Andre interrupted.

'Are you OK?' Raf asked softly.

Billie nodded. 'Yes, I am now. I had a bit of a bad day yesterday.'

'We heard all about it,' Andre said.

'I can't believe you threw your lunch over Cassandra!' Tilly said. 'I wish I'd seen it.'

'I can't believe you are not in the show,' Raf said.

Billie sighed. 'I know. That's why I turned my phone off. I didn't really feel up to speaking to anyone. Well, that and it's my mum and dad's wedding anniversary.'

'What, you like to hang around with your Ps on their special day?' Tilly asked.

'Don't you think that might be cramping their style?' Andre said.

Billie shook her head. 'No – my dad's, um . . .'

'Oh, man, I'm sorry, I forgot . . .' Andre said.

'It's OK, it's just that my mum always finds it hard.'

'I totally understand,' Tilly said.

'Me too,' Andre said. 'It's just like me and my dad.'

'Is he dead too?' Billie stared at him.

'No, but he might as well be,' Andre replied. 'He's dead to me.'

'Oh stop being such a drama queen,' Tilly said, nudging him.

'I think maybe we should go – leave you to be with your mum,' Raf said.

'No way!' Andre said. 'Remember why we came here?'

'Why did you come here?' Billie asked.

'Well, obviously, the main reason was because we were worried about you,' Andre said. 'But also we came to tell you that we need you.'

'What do you mean?'

'In the crew,' Tilly explained.

'It's just not the same without you,' Andre said.

'It really isn't,' Raf added.

'No,' said MJ, causing Tilly and Andre to turn round in shock, as if they'd forgotten he was there.

'See, even MJ says he misses you and you know he's a man of few words,' Andre said. 'So can we come in or what?'

Billie stared at him. 'What, into the flat?'

'No, into that spaceship over there,' Andre said sarcastically. 'Of course into the flat, you fool!'

'Billie, is everything OK?' her mum called from the living room.

'Is that your mum?' Andre asked.

Billie nodded.

'Don't worry, we're just some friends of Billie's

from WEDA,' Andre called. 'Is it OK if we come in?'

'Andre!' Tilly said.

Andre frowned at her. 'What? If you don't ask, you don't get.'

'Of course,' Billie's mum said, appearing in the living-room doorway. 'What a lovely surprise.'

To Billie's relief she looked genuinely pleased to see them.

One by one, the crew filed past Billie into the hallway.

'2013 called,' Andre said as he walked past her. 'It says it wants its tiger onesie back.'

'Very funny,' Billie said with a grin.

'It's so good to see you,' Tilly said, grabbing her in a hug.

'You too,' Billie said.

'Hey. I missed you today, in the stable,' Raf said gruffly. 'It wasn't the same without you.'

'Thank you.' Billie looked away as her face flushed.

'I'm very sorry you got taken out of the showcase,' MJ said. Then he gave her a half hug at arm's length.

Billie followed them into the living room. It was so weird seeing Il Bello in her flat. Weird but really nice.

'Can I get you guys anything?' her mum said. 'And please excuse the dressing gown, we were having a duvet day.'

'You're excused,' Andre said with a grin. 'Although that robe would look so much better with a string of pearls. And possibly a turban.'

'Do you think?' Billie's mum laughed.

'So, what do you say?' Andre turned to Billie. 'Will you come back to the crew?'

Billie sighed. It was so nice to see them all – and see how much they cared – she felt like she'd be crazy saying no. And she was out of the showcase now, so she didn't really have anything to lose. She'd no longer be breaking Miss Murphy's golden rule of no extra-curricular dance projects before a show. 'OK,' she said.

'Yes!' Tilly exclaimed.

Raf whooped and MJ did a pencil spin and moonwalked over to him for a high five.

'Awesome,' Andre said. 'Let's rehearse.'

Billie stared at him. 'What? Now?'

'Uh-huh. No time like the present – even though I hate that saying.'

'But I'm spending today with my mum.'

'I meant here,' Andre said. 'If that's OK with you, Mrs Edmonds.'

'Of course!' Billie's mum exclaimed. 'I'd love to see you guys dance.' She grinned at Billie. 'It'll be like watching a dance movie in 3D.'

Billie smiled. 'OK, if you're sure.'

The crew set about moving the furniture back against the walls, then Billie's mum snuggled back under her duvet on the sofa and Andre plugged his iPod into the stereo.

'How about we do some more work on our three Bs moves – try to put them into a routine?' he said.

At first, Billie felt super self-conscious, street

dancing in front of her mum, but then she closed her eyes and focused her attention on her body. Almost immediately she felt a rush of relief as her torso loosened and the pounding rhythm took over. She felt all of the tension being shaken from her limbs and she felt powerful, grounded and strong. She could be fearless. She could be real. Street dancing showed her how.

Billie broke from choreography with Andre and Tilly and strutted fiercely over to Raf. They made eye contact and he placed her hands around his neck. She heard her mum whoop with delight as he lifted her up.

For the next hour they worked on fitting their signature moves together into a routine. When they'd finally cracked it the crew had a group hug.

'That was fierce!' Tilly gasped.

'You guys are amazing,' Billie's mum said, getting to her feet. 'And you must be really hungry. Let me make you something to eat.'

'Are you sure?' Billie asked.

Her mum smiled, her face glowing. Billie hadn't seen her look so happy in ages. 'Of course. It's the least I could do after putting on a show like that. You're all so talented.'

The crew chorused their thank yous.

'Your mum's so cool,' Tilly said, after she'd gone into the kitchen.

'Yeah. Not everyone could pull off that towelling robe look so well,' Andre quipped.

Billie burst out laughing. Today had been amazing. She looked over at the photo of her and her dad that had been on the dream-board and was now placed on the book shelf.

'Thank you,' she said to him silently, before joining the rest of the crew on the sofa.

CHAPTER FIFTEEN

The next day in Maths, Tilly came rushing over to Billie, her eyes gleaming with excitement and her fingers flecked with paint.

'I started another mural last night,' she said. 'On the other stable wall. I can't wait for you to see it.'

Billie grinned. Tilly's excitement was infectious. 'What's it of?'

Tilly shook her head. 'You'll have to wait and see.'

As Billie turned to get her books out of her bag she saw Cassandra sitting at the table behind, staring at them. Billie looked away. From now on she was going to act as if Cassandra didn't exist. Cassandra wanted to annoy her and get her into trouble. But there was no way Billie was going to fall for that again.

'I can't wait till lunchtime,' she whispered to Tilly.

'I know. Our routine is sick!'

As usual at lunchtime, Billie and Tilly went to the stable separately, with Billie waiting for Tilly to go first. The sky above was bright blue and the crisp autumn leaves crunched beneath her feet as she made her way through the trees. Even though she was still really disappointed not to be in the showcase, Billie felt as if a weight had lifted from her shoulders. Things were so much better with her mum and she loved being part of Il Bello. She snuck around the back of the stable and through the door, feeling happy and light.

The others were all gathered around Tilly's new mural.

'Billie, take a look at this,' Andre said.

'She has created a masterpiece,' Raf said with a grin.

MJ looked at Billie and nodded.

Billie joined them and gazed up at the wall.

Tilly had drawn each of them performing their signature three Bs moves.

'Tilly! This is amazing!' Billie exclaimed.

Tilly's face flushed and all of her swagger dissolved away, leaving a shy smile in its place. 'Do you think so?'

'I know so,' Billie said. 'You're so cool.'

'Yeah well, don't big her up too much,' Andre said. 'Her head might get too big for dancing.'

'Speaking of dancing,' Raf said, 'can we please try our routine again?'

'Yes!' Tilly exclaimed.

MJ moonwalked over to the dance floor.

'I've come up with something we can all do at the end,' Andre said. 'Look.'

They all watched as he fanned his fingers around his face.

'It's sign language for beautiful. Beautiful – Il Bello – get it?'

'Cool,' Tilly said as she copied him. 'It's like voguing.'

'Well, if it's good enough for Madonna . . .' Andre said with a grin. 'Come on, guys, show me you're beautiful!'

As Billie practised the Il Bello move she thought about the word beautiful. For so long she'd thought it was something external, something that was only skin deep. But when she danced with Il Bello she felt beautiful from the inside out.

'OK, let's take it from the top,' Andre called, selecting their track on the iPod and counting them in. 'Five, six, seven, eight, snap.'

Billie felt the beat enter her body, starting in her chest and working its way through her limbs. She rocked her spine back and forth before jumping into some high knees house moves. And once again the sense of freedom that street dancing brought washed through her.

'Remember the three Bs,' Tilly called.

As Billie lost herself in the rhythm she could no longer tell where her body ended and the music began. It was as if she *was* the music. And she was real, fearless and authentic. They all were. Raf started doing some freestyle partnering with her, supporting her flexy moves with swagger. She felt such a connection with the floor, so grounded as he spun her and directed her around. She had swagger. Now that they all had their moves down and no longer had to think about what to do, there was a new energy in the crew. It felt wild and exciting and raw.

'Vogue with an Il Bello twist!' Andre called as the track came to an end.

The crew jumped into formation and performed a flawless signature move.

'Boom shakalaka!' Andre cried.

'That was on point!' Tilly said.

Billie put her hands on her hips and tried to get her breath back.

'You were awesome,' Raf said, smiling.

MJ spun round and threw his hat in the air.

There was a loud cough from the doorway and they all froze.

'Would somebody please explain to me what is going on?' Miss Murphy said, a deep frown etched into her face.

'Uh-oh,' Andre muttered. 'Houston, we may have a problem.'

'Well?' Miss Murphy said, coming into the stable and looking around. Her eyes fell on Tilly's mural and for a moment she looked pleasantly surprised. Then she frowned again and came over to the crew. 'Do you not remember my two golden rules? Working on extra-curricular dance is banned in the run-up to a big show. All of you are taking part in the showcase . . . apart from Billie.'

Billie's heart sank as Miss Murphy looked at her. She couldn't bring herself to meet her gaze and see disappointment there yet again. Then she looked at Tilly's mural of them dancing and a burst of determination cut through her fear. Il Bello were supposed to be all about being fearless and authentic – maybe if they showed Miss Murphy what they'd been doing she'd feel differently.

'Why don't we show her our routine?' Billie said. She turned to Miss Murphy. 'Please, we've been working really hard on this. I think you'll like it.'

'Oh, do you?' Miss Murphy said, her face completely expressionless.

Billie turned to Andre but even he looked apprehensive. Tilly was looking at the floor. 'Come on,' Billie urged, 'The three Bs, remember.'

'And what, may I ask, are the three Bs?' Miss Murphy said.

'Be you, be fearless, be authentic,' Billie replied.

'It's our ethos,' Tilly muttered.

'Is it now?' Miss Murphy replied, but her frown had softened slightly. 'Go on then, show me what this is all about.'

The crew gathered in a quick huddle.

'This is our one chance,' Billie whispered.

'We're going to have to knock it out of the park,' Andre desperately whispered. 'Trust me. We are going to have to dance for your lives if we want to win her round.'

The group broke apart and they all took their places. Miss Murphy stepped back to watch.

'Five, six, seven, eight, snap,' Andre counted. And then they were off again. And, because they'd just done the routine, once Billie got over her initial nerves about Miss Murphy watching, she felt even more fearless and wild than before. She could tell it was the same for the others too. Each one of them performed their signature moves with more passion than ever. They really were dancing as if their lives depended on it. Then the track came to an end and they performed the Il Bello Street Crew sign.

After what seemed like an eternity, Miss Murphy finally spoke. 'Who choreographed this dance?'

'We all did,' Andre replied.

Miss Murphy looked visibly shocked. Billie couldn't tell if this was a good or bad thing.

'We've been rehearsing most lunchtimes,' Andre said.

'Very enterprising,' Miss Murphy replied drily.

'Look, I know you think street dance doesn't

have a place at WEDA but can't you see now that it does?' Andre said imploringly. 'You always tell us to never say "I can't",' he continued. 'You always talk about believing in ourselves and following our passions. Well, street dance is my passion. Please, Mum. I need it in my life and not just as a hobby – as a real form of expression.'

Miss Murphy started walking towards the door. 'All of you get your things together and see me in my office.'

'But, Mum –' Andre called after her.

'*Now*, Andre,' she replied before walking out of the door.

All the way back to the main building Billie's stomach felt like lead. Although she hadn't broken Miss Murphy's golden rule, she'd helped the others to and maybe in Miss Murphy's eyes that was just as bad. As the main entrance loomed into view Billie felt sick. What if she was about to get expelled? What if, after finally achieving her dream of coming to WEDA she got expelled in the very first term? As they silently trooped through the reception area Billie saw Cassandra hovering by the water cooler.

'Looks like someone just got busted,' Cassandra muttered as Billie walked past.

Billie gulped. Was Cassandra behind this too? Had she seen them going to the stable? Had she reported them? But as Billie followed the others up the long corridor she couldn't even bring herself to get angry. She was way too anxious about what was about to happen.

'Come in and close the door,' Miss Murphy said as they all nervously edged into her office. 'First of all,' she began, 'you should never have been using the stable without permission.'

'But we –' Andre began.

Miss Murphy held up her hand to silence him. 'Please, let me finish. You should never have used the stable because it might not be safe. That building hasn't been used in years. We would need to do a proper health and safety inspection before you can use it again.'

'Use it again?' Andre echoed.

'Yes. So in the meantime, you're to use the Fontaine Studio. I think it's free most lunchtimes.'

'We're allowed to use a studio?' Tilly asked.

'To street dance?' Andre said, his eyes wide with shock.

Miss Murphy nodded. 'How else are you going to get enough practice for the showcase?'

'The showcase?' Billie stared at her, confused.

'Yes. I'd like you to perform the routine you just showed me.'

'OK, what have you done with my mother?' Andre said, laughing. 'You look like her and you frown like her but you definitely aren't talking like her!'

Miss Murphy leaned back in her chair and smiled. 'I was blown away by the heart and soul you all just poured into that dance. I think it will make a very exciting addition to the showcase and a great example of the passion for dance we try to encourage at WEDA.'

Raf and Andre high-fived and MJ grinned. Tilly hooked her arm through Billie's and squeezed her tight.

'A good dancer never stops learning,' Miss Murphy said. 'Not even when she becomes a teacher. You all taught me a valuable lesson today. Now, if you'll excuse me, I have work to do.'

The crew spilled out into the corridor, laughing and cheering.

'Oh my God, your mum is awesome!' Tilly cried.

Andre smiled proudly. 'Where do you think I get it from?'

As they came down the stairs Billie spotted Cassandra hanging around near the lockers. When she saw them all laughing she looked shocked. Billie sighed. She still couldn't be bothered to get angry with her. If she had snitched on them, she'd ended up doing them a massive favour. Especially Billie. Not only had she not been expelled, she was back in the showcase – and doing something she loved, with people she really cared about. None of the crew would try to block her or ruin her dance like Cassandra would. They were her true friends and they had her back. Billie felt her phone vibrate in her pocket.

'I'll catch you guys up,' she said to the others.

It was a text from her mum. Billie felt a brief wave of panic. What if she was feeling sad again? But her mum had sent her a photo. It was of a handwritten message, written by Billie's dad – she recognized the handwriting instantly.

You inspire me with your determination. I love you.

Billie scrolled down to the message from her mum.

I found this today when I was clearing out some stuff. Your father sent it to me years ago but I think he'd want you to have it now. He'd be so inspired by you, Billie – just as I am. I'm so proud to be your mum xxxx

Billie gulped as she looked back at her dad's words. Then she had a thought that filled her with happiness. Maybe when the people you loved died they weren't really gone for good. They kept finding ways to let you know that they loved you . . . and they always would.

CHAPTER SIXTEEN

'Did you know that in Arabia they used to believe that stories flowed like streams underground?' Uncle Charlie paused to take a sip of his tea.

Billie stared at him across the cafe table. He was just back from his construction job in Dubai and was even more tanned than ever. 'What do you mean?'

'They believed that all stories already exist, they're just looking for people who will tell them. So every time someone thinks to themselves that they'd like to write a story, that story comes rushing to them like an underground stream and bubbles up through their pen – or keyboard I guess, nowadays,' Charlie added with a chuckle.

Billie thought about all of her favourite stories racing about underground trying to find someone to tell them and she smiled. 'I love that idea.'

'Me too.' Charlie grinned.

'Do you think it's the same for poems?'

'I don't see why not.'

Billie reached down inside her bag. 'Your poem helped me so much this first term at WEDA.'

'Really?' Charlie looked chuffed. 'That's great.'

'So I thought to say thank you I'd write you one of my own.' Billie pulled a folded piece of paper from her bag. 'It's called "The Daring Dreamer". It's about you.'

'Love it!' Charlie took the poem and began to read.

Billie looked over to the counter where her mum was busy plating up a freshly baked batch of mince pies. Her favourite Jill Scott album was playing on the stereo and she was humming along. In the past few weeks it was as if her mum had got all her colour back. Her hair was gleaming and her cheeks were glowing.

'Billerina, this is beautiful.' Uncle Charlie put the poem down and looked at her. His eyes were shining like he was close to tears. 'Thank you.'

The door of the cafe opened, bringing with it a cold burst of air. 'Special delivery coming through,' Tony called. At least, Billie thought it was Tony; she could barely see him beneath the huge Christmas tree he was carrying.

'Where do you want it, boss?' he called to Billie's mum.

'Oh, Tony, it's perfect!' Kate cried. She gestured to the space by the condiments counter Billie had helped her clear earlier. 'How can I repay you?' she said, coming over to help Tony set up the tree.

Tony shook his head. 'No need to repay me – your expertly brewed tea is repayment enough.'

Billie's mum giggled.

'Aye aye,' Charlie said under his breath. 'Do I detect the first budding signs of a romance?'

Billie grinned. 'I don't know, but I hope so.' And she truly did. Her mum deserved to be happy again and Tony clearly thought the world of her.

'So, how are you feeling then?' Uncle Charlie asked. 'Any last-minute nerves?'

Billie nodded. 'Yes, but I'm excited too. I can't believe I'm going to be dancing at the Albert Hall!'

'The *Royal* Albert Hall,' Charlie corrected. 'I can't believe I'm related to someone who's going to be dancing there! You're gonna be great, Bill. I'm not the only Daring Dreamer, you know.'

'I'd better get going,' Billie said, gathering her things together. 'I absolutely cannot be late for this.'

'Are you off, love?' Billie's mum called as Billie put on her coat.

'Yes. Wish me luck.'

'You don't need it,' her mum said, coming over and wrapping Billie in a hug.

Billie breathed in the familiar scent of her perfume and baking. As always, it felt so reassuring.

'I can't wait to see you up on that stage,' her mum said, smiling at her proudly.

'Yeah, good luck, Billie. I can't wait to hear all about it,' Tony said.

'Oh, you will be hearing all about it,' her mum said with a grin. 'I have a feeling I won't be talking about anything else for months!'

When Billie arrived at the stage door for the Royal Albert Hall, her heart was thudding so loud she could hardly hear herself think. The man on the door directed her downstairs to a corridor which ran all the way around the basement of the circular hall. Billie thought of all the famous dancers and musicians who'd walked along there before her and her heart thudded even louder. Finally, she reached the door to the dressing room she'd been directed to. A printed sign had been stuck to the door: *WEDA SHOWCASE – IL BELLO STREET CREW*. As Billie opened the door she had a flashback to the first time she'd opened the old stable door to meet with Andre and the rest of the crew. She'd been so nervous back then, so apprehensive about street dance. If someone had told her then that she'd end up doing it at the Royal Albert Hall she would never have believed them.

'Oh, Billie, thank God!' Andre exclaimed as she walked in. 'There's been a major crisis!'

Billie's heart plummeted. Was one of the crew injured? Had Miss Murphy had a last-minute change of mind? Was street dancing banned at the Royal Albert Hall? 'What is it?' she said, her voice trembling.

'I've totally ruined my eyebrows, look!' Andre came over and shoved his face in hers. Instead of arching right down over his eyes, his brows were now only about a centimetre long.

'Is that it?' Billie said, flooded with relief. 'I thought something really bad had happened.'

'Something really bad *has* happened!' Andre exclaimed. 'Look at me – I'm maimed for life!'

'Er, I'm pretty sure eyebrows grow back, so you're only maimed for now. Who did it to you?'

'That's the worst part.' Andre collapsed down on

to the wooden bench that ran along one side of the dressing room. '*I* did it to me. It was meant to be a statement.'

'What kind of statement?'

'A fashion statement. But it ended up being a fashion disaster. I can never go out in public again.'

Billie put down her bag and took off her coat.

'Oh, you look amazing!' Andre said.

'Do I?' Billie felt a burst of relief. When she'd been getting ready earlier she'd put some violet sparkle across the tops of her cheekbones and experimented with plaiting her hair. She was wearing a black leotard with black mesh through the shoulders and sleeves, and a mesh hoodie with reflective pops of light saying *Be fearless* on the back. She'd finished the outfit off with a pair of glossy black high-top tennis shoes that Tilly had lent her.

'Great. Even *you* have more swag than me now,' Andre said, slumping back on the bench.

Billie chose to ignore him. Andre was clearly in

a highly emotional state. 'OK, calm down, I'm sure there'll be a solution.'

'A solution to what?' Tilly said, coming in. She was wearing a jewelled captain's hat and a marching-band jacket over her leotard. Her bobbed hair was bleached snowy-white and she'd painted her lips pastel purple and pink.

'Oh my God, guys, can you believe we're actually here?' Tilly's mouth fell open in shock. 'Andre, what happened to your face?'

'See, I told you!' Andre said, looking at Billie accusingly. 'I'm going to be a laughing stock.'

'Who did this to you?' Tilly said fiercely, like she was squaring up for a fight.

'Oh don't *you* ask,' Andre said with a dramatic sigh. 'I did it, OK? And now I need to undo it. Only I can't.' He slumped forwards, his head in his hands.

Tilly looked at him and shook her head. 'Seriously? You pick the day we're performing at the Albert Hall to exterminate your eyebrows?' She sighed and pulled her huge make-up bag from her backpack. 'Don't worry. I can fix them.'

'You can?' Andre sat bolt upright and looked at her hopefully.

'Yep.' Tilly started sorting through her cosmetics. 'Lucky for you I have a load of eyebrow pencils.'

'Oh, you're my saviour!' Andre exclaimed just as Raf and MJ walked through the door.

'Thank goodness,' Raf said, with a grin.

'I'm just going to use the bathroom,' Billie said and she slipped back out into the corridor.

While she was inside a cubicle she heard the bathroom door open, and a woman's voice cut through the silence.

'I cannot believe you have put on two pounds right before the showcase,' the woman said. She had a strong Eastern European accent and her voice sounded really familiar, but Billie wasn't sure where she knew it from.

'How many times do you want me to say sorry?' a girl replied. Cassandra! Billie froze.

'I am putting you on a diet over Christmas,'

Cassandra's mum said. 'We are going to get you back in shape before the new term.'

Billie frowned. Cassandra was one of the thinnest girls at the academy. She'd hardly ever seen her eating anything more than an apple. No wonder she was so uptight about her food, if this was how her mum treated her. No wonder she was so uptight, full stop. For the first time since meeting her, Billie felt a pang of sympathy for Cassandra. She waited until she heard them both go into cubicles then quickly slipped out, washed her hands and left.

Back in the dressing room, Il Bello were huddled together in a group hug. Raf and Tilly parted to let Billie join them. As she felt their arms around her she felt filled with strength.

'This is it, guys,' Andre said. Tilly had done an expert job of filling in his eyebrows, Billie noticed to her relief. 'This is our big chance to shine and share the ethos of the three Bs.'

A bell rang three times through the tannoy in the ceiling.

'Three minutes till curtain up,' Andre said. 'OK, let's do this!'

The stage in the Albert Hall was in the centre of the round hall. As Billie and the rest of Il Bello waited in the wings, she felt sick with nerves. Even Raf, who normally looked so laidback, was playing with his beads anxiously. Billie pictured her mum and Uncle Charlie sitting somewhere in the huge auditorium. And she pictured her dad, standing right behind her. 'You've got this, Billie,' she imagined him whispering. 'I'm so proud of you.' She took a deep breath as the act before them came to a close and the hall erupted in cheers.

'And up next,' the compere called, 'we have Il Bello!'

Billie and the others made their way up the aisle towards the stage. Her face burned as the audience turned to look at them . There were so many people! What if she forgot her moves? What if she messed up? What if she let the crew down? But as soon as they got on to the stage and the house lights dimmed, she was able to pull her focus back to Il Bello. *Just pretend you're back in the stable*, she told herself. *Pretend no one's watching*. But then another inner voice, a stronger inner voice said, *No, you're not in a stable, you're in the Royal Albert Hall. Own it. Be fearless. Be real*. Billie took a deep breath.

The energy from the massive crowd was electric. She felt it crackling through every fibre in her body. *This is it*, Billie told herself, *everything you've worked for, all of the training – it's all brought you to here*.

The beat hit and the crew exploded into life.

The routine went by in a blur but every big move was nailed and everyone was completely in sync. At the end the crew got into formation and pulled their signature Il Bello move. The lights dropped, there was a moment's silence . . . and then the crowd went wild! As the cheers erupted they all gasped for air. Sweat trickled down Billie's face and she felt a power inside of her so strong she felt as if she could pick up the entire building and everyone inside. This must be what Mr Marlo meant when he talked about finding their 'inner dance warrior'. She'd finally discovered her street beast within.

'Oh my God, they love us!' Tilly exclaimed as the crew flung their arms round each other and took a bow.

'Of course they do!' Andre yelled. 'We're awesome.'

'Even without the eyebrows,' Raf said, winking at Billie.

Billie looked out into the sea of faces, searching for her mum and Uncle Charlie. There were so many people there it was impossible to tell. But then she saw someone jumping up and down, waving his hands in the air. It was Charlie. And there was her mum, leaping up and down beside him, looking equally excited. Billie felt as if she might burst with joy. After taking their bows to every side of the hall the crew ran from the stage, the crowd still cheering. Miss Murphy was waiting for them in the wings.

'I'm so proud of you,' she said. 'You've done

WEDA proud. And I have some news that I think will make you very happy.'

They all looked at her expectantly.

'When you come back after Christmas, street dance will be on the curriculum.'

'Seriously?' Andre stared at her.

'Yes. You've shown me that it deserves to be. And you will be dancing in the brand new Stable Studio.' Miss Murphy smiled at them.

'The Stable Studio?' Andre repeated incredulously. 'Do you mean *the* stable?'

Miss Murphy nodded. 'It's being refurbished over the break.' She turned to Tilly. 'We're keeping your awesome artwork though.'

Tilly stared at her. 'OK, I think I must be dreaming. Real life is never this good!'

Miss Murphy laughed.

The crew all looked at each other for a moment, then, as the reality of what Miss Murphy had just told them began to sink in, they started jumping up and down with excitement.

'I've got to get back for the final performance,' Miss Murphy said. 'Why don't you guys take your celebrations back to your dressing room, so you don't disturb anyone?'

'Thanks so much, Mum,' Andre said, hugging Miss Murphy tight.

'You're very welcome.' Miss Murphy stared at him. 'Goodness, Andre! What has happened to your eyebrows?'

Tilly looked at Andre as he gasped in horror. 'Oh, whoops. You've sweated off the pencil.'

'My life is over!' Andre exclaimed.

'I think you'll find that it isn't,' MJ said dryly.

'Haha, go, MJ!' Tilly laughed.

Andre looked at Billie and sighed. 'Why did I bother trying to get him to talk more if he's just going to be insolent?'

Billie laughed as Andre dragged Tilly back towards the dressing room. 'Paint them back before someone sees me,' he cried.

'So, it was pretty awesome just now, no?' Raf said,

falling into step with Billie. Beads of sweat were trickling down the sides of his face and he looked happier than she'd ever seen him.

Billie nodded. 'It was amazing.' Her skin was still tingling with excitement and it felt as if her heart was pumping raw courage around her body. As Billie looked along the empty corridor she suddenly had an idea. 'Wait there,' she said to Raf and MJ. Then she took a deep breath, ran a few steps, launched her body over . . . and performed a perfect aerial cartwheel. As Raf and MJ whooped and laughed Billie thought of Mr Marlo. Finally she got what he'd been trying to teach her. If you wanted something to happen you had to truly believe that it would.

After they'd all got hot chocolates from the vending machine in the corridor outside, they returned to the dressing room and sat in a circle on the floor.

'To Il Bello!' Andre said, raising his cup.

'To Il Bello,' the others echoed.

'To keeping it real,' Tilly said.

'To keeping it real.' The others raised their drinks again.

'And to being fearless,' Raf said.

'To being fearless.'

'To Michael Jackson,' MJ said.

'What?' They all looked at him.

'He's my inspiration,' MJ said defiantly.

'OK,' said Andre, raising his cup. 'To Michael Jackson.'

Billie took a sip of her hot chocolate. It felt like velvet on her tongue. She thought back once again to the first time she'd gone to the stable and how she'd been convinced she didn't have what it takes to street dance. It had never felt so good to be proved wrong.

'To never saying "I can't",' she said, raising her drink.

'To never saying "I can't",' the others said loudly, their voices echoing around the room, reverberating around Billie's rib cage, and filling her with hope.

THE PERFORMANCE

by Billie Edmonds

Warm sunshine breeze
Blowing through my veins.
Living in the moment,
I'm content,
Free from worries,
Dreaming in colour.
Dance keeps me from hiding in darkness,
It helps me step into the light,
I'm breathing in the world around me,
Oxygen cleanses my soul
Bringing me back to love.
A rainbow of reflections
Inspires me along the way.
In waves of emotion,
Imperfections shine through.
Living the dream is my reality,
Whirlwinds take me away,
But smiling faces reassure me –

What's passed is past, is done.
And I am me, as weird as can be
And so I choose to be FREE!

Be you, be fearless, be authentic

TILLY'S TIME TO SHINE

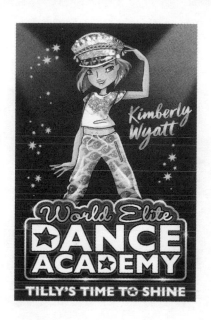

Fashionista Tilly has never fitted in –
her unique sense of style, her overflowing
creativity and her 'attitude problem' means that
she's not the average WEDA student. But Tilly is
struggling with things hardly anyone knows about –
and they're affecting her dancing and school work.

Will Tilly find a way to overcome
her frustrations and keep her grades up?
Or is her WEDA dream over?

COMING SOON!